CW00537040

HAUNTED TALES

HAUNTED TALES

*Ghostly stories for the
darkest nights*

ADAM MACQUEEN

Swift

SWIFT PRESS

First published in Great Britain by Swift Press 2024

1 3 5 7 9 8 6 4 2

Typesetting and text design by Tetragon, London
Printed and bound in Great Britain by CPI Group (UK) Ltd, Croydon, CRO 4YY

A CIP catalogue record for this book is available from the British Library

ISBN: 9781800754454
eISBN: 9781800754461

*For my mum, Sandra Macqueen, who
collected my ghost stories proudly together,
while never believing a word of them.*

*1937–2023
and after*

CONTENTS

This side of the darkest meadows
I'll make my winter dwelling
And there
I'll crush my bones

'HOT MEAT', THE SUGARCUBES, 1989

THE WRONG
TELETUBBY

RICHARD'S son stopped speaking to him a week after he died.

He had got into the habit of logging in to Facebook first thing every morning, when the weight of what had happened made it difficult to do anything, just to see once more the last thing his son would ever say to him.

Luke Davies cant wait to hit the surf this w/e!!!!!
23 October 2010 at 23:08
Comment/Like

And then, on the day of Luke's funeral, after Richard stood and watched his child disappear impossibly into the ground, he got home and fired up the computer only to find he had taken his final message with him. Luke's face was still there, grinning out of some overcrowded freshers' week bar crawl, complete with the remnants of his gap-year tan and the wispy beginnings of a goatee beard Richard had never got to see in real life. And his name was still there, and the photos he was tagged in that had become so familiar, and the news that he had changed his location to Loughborough and become a member of Loughborough University and the Department of Modern Languages and the Athletics Soc and the Indie Soc and the Windsurfing Soc, and he was attending Fresh 'n' Wild at the Union and the Poly Bop in the Cellar Bar and was now friends with dozens of people Richard had never heard of. And there was even a message from the very same day from someone called Hal Barnett asking if *NE1 got spare car space down to Plym on sat??????*, but his status update was gone. Kaput. Disappeared. His son had gone silent.

Richard supposed they just cleared themselves after a while. Now he thought about it, he had put one up when he first joined – *Richard Davies is not sure about this new-fangled technology!* or some such – and that wasn't there any more, even though he didn't remember deleting it. He only had a handful of friends – he'd only really joined the thing because Luke had said it would be a good way for them to keep in touch after he went to uni – and most of them never bothered to update their status things either, apart from Bob at work who seemed to put some rubbish about what he was eating or doing or watching on telly every couple of hours, till Richard had even thought about deleting him as a friend except he knew he would notice.

He sat staring at the computer screen for so long that the white light that bleached his face dropped to a dull grey and then switched itself off completely, and he became aware of the shadows and the cold around him and the fact that he hadn't switched on a single light in the house, let alone the central heating. He twitched the mouse to bring the computer back to life, and accidentally managed to click on one of the links in front of him on Luke's page: the Windsurfing Soc.

And he was so glad he had. The first thing he saw beneath the logo was a message from someone called Alistair Thorne. He remembered an Alistair from the funeral: a nice lad, he had come over to talk to him and Luke's mother specially.

As many of you know, the society suffered a terrible loss last weekend when Luke Davies, one of our newest members, drowned in a freak accident at the BUCS event in Plymouth. I know all members will join me in passing on the society's deepest condolences to his friends and family.

A party from the university will be attending his funeral in Guildford this Saturday at 3pm; I will be going on behalf of the society. There are still places in the minibus for any

of Luke's friends who would like to attend – contact Dr
Buckland for details.

I've also started **this tribute page** for those who will
not be able to attend so they can leave their memories
of Luke.

Richard clicked on the link and let out a sound that was
somewhere between a gasp and a sob: here was his son
again, in a photo he had not seen before, in his wetsuit,
grinning and waving at the camera on a shingle beach
with sails in the background. The beard was a lot more
impressive. This must have been taken on the day the
accident happened. It was like he had been given another
chance to see him.

He scrolled down, his eyes misting as he read through
the messages beneath. There were dozens of them.

I only knew Luke a few weeks but he was one of the
nicest people to me in the first week, showing me how
to work the cooker in our kitchen and rescuing me in the
bar more than once like a true gentleman! I can't believe
he is gone and I will miss him so much

I was at school with Luke for five years and was lookin
forward to seeing him at xmas. Can't believe I will never
see him again. He was such a great bloke, neva had a bad

word for anyone and was a real team player – we played
rugby together in the First XV that took the Charter cup
for the first time in four years. But more than that he was
a great laugh and a superb guy. RIP buddy

RIP Big Man. Never see his like again

Just heard the news I am so gutted. Raced against Luke
many times but only managed to beat him once – and
that was because he was having treatment on his ankle
at the time! He was a true sportsman – one in a million.

He recognised some of the names; one or two of the pic-
tures looked familiar. But there were so many people here
he had never heard of, people from around the country,
around the world, even – there was a chap here writing
from Malaysia – and his son had touched every one of
their lives enough that they had come here to pay their
respects to him.

Richard left the computer to blow his nose, splash water
on his face and get himself a whisky. He wasn't certain
he actually liked whisky, but he generally had a bottle in
for occasions that demanded it, and this was surely one
of them.

Once he had located the bit where you could leave a
message – he knew it was right because a little picture of

himself came up beside it – he took a good twenty minutes or more to compose it properly, half worrying that there would be a deadline on these too and it would go out there half-finished, making him look demented. In the end he kept it simple:

> Hello everyone, this is Luke's dad. Just wanted to say how much these messages mean to me and our family. Luke was so loved and touched so many people wherever he went. I will miss my son so much but it is a great comfort to me to come to this page and read all your memories of him. Thank you all from the bottom of my heart.

He took out the bit about 'our family' before he pressed Comment. Denise had always hated him speaking for her. He sent her the link to the tribute page instead. She was on Facebook – though she kept some of her pages protected – but he wasn't sure to send links that way, so he ended up emailing it to her instead.

After that he sat up looking through Luke's photo albums for a few more hours until he'd finished the whisky and he suddenly realised it was three in the morning and he still hadn't switched the central heating on.

When he checked the page the next evening three of Luke's friends had added messages after his one. He didn't recognise any of the names, but it was very nice of them all to send their condolences.

He went on checking the page every morning before he went into work. It did him good to see Luke's grinning face first thing, gave him something to get out of bed for, and he could hardly look at it in the office after what he'd said to the youngsters about not using Facebook or Twitter or any of the other ones during working hours. Besides, if he started looking at it at work he wasn't sure he'd ever be able to do anything else.

On the Tuesday there was a short message from Denise at the bottom of the page – *As Luke's mother it gives me great strength to read the messages here thank you all god bless xx* – so he knew she'd got the email. She hadn't written anything back to him, but the counsellor had said there would probably be elements of blaming the other, and it wasn't exactly as if they'd been having many civil conversations before the accident. Although he had to admit she'd been a tower of strength at the funeral.

Towards the end of the week he got a private message. He knew because a little icon he'd never noticed at the top of the page lit up red and when he clicked on it, it said he had a message from someone called Sadie. She was a friend of Luke's from university – the girl he had helped with the cooker – and she said how sorry she was not just about his death but not to have had a chance to talk to Richard at the funeral as well. She told him a bit more about what Luke had been like at university. Apparently a whole bunch of them had gone back to his room on the first night after the bar had closed and he had cooked everyone cheese toasties and made so much tea that she had felt guilty and taken him round some of her spare teabags the next day and they had been good friends from then on. She wasn't on the same course as him but they'd hung out, as she put it, lots ever since, and she'd seen him just the night before he went off on the windsurfing trip and how excited he was about it and how he'd shown her his new wetsuit and his equipment all laid out and ready to be packed.

It wasn't clear from the message whether they'd been boyfriend and girlfriend, but Richard got the impression she might have liked to have been. Whichever way, it wasn't for him to ask, so when he wrote back he tried to keep it quite chatty and said how nice it was of her to get in touch and how much he appreciated it, and how it helped to hear about how happy Luke had been in the weeks before he had died and everything he'd been up to. And then he said, please keep in touch if you'd like to, and she wrote back and said that would be nice and then added in an apologetic sort of PS that she'd already been down to visit her own parents twice since Luke had died even though at the beginning of term she couldn't wait to get away, but losing him made her feel totally different and more appreciative of each day and what she had. And he wrote back to her and said if that was the lesson that Luke's friends took away from him dying then perhaps something good could come from it after all, and when he switched the computer off there was a part of him that really believed it. Which was progress.

The lad from the windsurfing club wrote to him too, a week or so later. His message was a bit more stilted and formal, but then the insurance claim and the investigation into the accident were still going through, so that was understandable, especially since he was writing partly in an official capacity to say that they were going to put up a commemorative panel in Luke's memory in their clubhouse, and he would very much like both Richard and Denise to come to the unveiling the following term if they were able. Richard wrote straight back and said he couldn't speak for his ex-wife but he would definitely be there, and he went out the next day and bought a diary for the following year to put the date in, which meant he was Looking Ahead like his counsellor had said, and that was definitely progress too.

Time passed. Mostly it seemed to go at a glacial pace. When a couple of pints that Mike and Eleanor dutifully insisted on taking him for in the Rose and Crown had loosened his tongue and his inhibitions, he admitted to them that it sometimes felt like he was wading through treacle. And then one day he looked up and noticed that the Christmas lights had gone up in the shopping precinct and it was more than a month since his son died.

He still checked Facebook every day. There hadn't been any more entries on the tribute page, and he knew all the old ones off by heart by now, but it still gave him comfort to read his favourite ones. He sometimes clicked through to Sadie's page just to see what she was up to, and she seemed to be getting on fine. She'd got a part in the end-of-term panto – she was studying Drama and English – and there were all sorts of messages from her other friends, but he felt a bit weird reading through them. He was sure she wouldn't mind him keeping an avuncular eye on her, but he drew the line at clicking on any of her photographs. Unless they were ones that Luke was tagged in, of course, but it wasn't like there was ever going to be any more of those.

And then, all of a sudden, there was. Not on Sadie's page, but around halfway down the main page you got when you logged in, lost among all the stuff about what Bob thought about last night's *Apprentice* and people inviting him to play Farmville or Golden Gems and the updates from Audi and Genesis Official and the golf club that he couldn't work out how to switch off. It was way down on the page, even though it said it had only been posted seven hours ago, and it was all he could do to keep his hand steady enough on the mouse to actually click on it.

He couldn't make head or tail of what he saw. It was just a black rectangle. It looked like, whoever had taken it, their flash hadn't gone off, or they'd pressed the button by mistake, but why would they bother to go through the faff of putting it up on Facebook, let alone tagging it with Luke's name? He moved the cursor around the picture to see where Luke was supposed to be, but the square that lit up with his name was just a dark patch in more darkness. He even tried turning the brightness right up on his screen, but it didn't help much. All you could see was a bit of what might be a chessboard, or a floor covered in black and white tiles, and the rest was all darkness and shadows.

He was hovering over the monitor, trying to look at it from a different angle that might help him make out more, when he spotted the tag and thumped down heavily into the protesting chair. He could taste bile in the back of his throat. He had been looking at the wrong thing.

Posted by Luke Davies, 11 December 2010

It was impossible. It was awful. It was grotesque.

When the hammering in his head had subsided enough for him to be able to think, he tried to convince himself it must just be a horrible coincidence. Could it be that there was another Luke Davies on Facebook, and he had stumbled across him because of crossed wires somewhere in the system? He was always getting things suggesting he become friends with all sorts of people he had never heard of. What if Facebook had just decided he ought to look at this person's photographs because they had the same surname?

No. He clicked on the name, and it took him to the familiar page with his son's smiling face still staring out from the top of it. And there it was again, at the top of his own page above all the familiar photos from months earlier, the little black rectangle with its impossible date.

He felt like he couldn't breathe. How could this be happening? It must be a mistake. It had to be. He forced himself to walk away from the computer and the black hole burning in the middle of the screen, went into the kitchen and poured himself a glass of ice-cold water which he made himself down in one. The glass skittered across the draining board when he put it down, his hands were shaking so much.

He forced himself to think about it logically. His son was dead. The fact that Facebook said it was Luke who had put the photograph there just meant someone had posted it using his account. They warned you every time you went on to it about not leaving yourself logged in, and that must be what had happened. Someone was using his computer, and he'd left his Facebook open – because why wouldn't he, it's not like he knew he wasn't coming back – and they'd accidentally put the photo up on his account rather than their own. It was a simple mistake, and they would probably be mortified when they realised.

Which would be a fine explanation, if he wasn't looking at his son's laptop right now. It was sitting in his bedroom on top of the boxes of things he had collected from the hall of residence the week after his death. He hadn't had the strength to go through them yet.

There could be another explanation. He went back to his own computer, averting his eyes from the inky blackness in the centre of the screen, and clicked through to Sadie's profile instead. He had three goes at writing a message to her before he gave up. Her mobile number was on there. It wasn't too late. Not for a student.

'Hello?' She took a while to pick up, probably wary of the unfamiliar number.

'Sadie? Hello. Sorry to phone you, it's Richard Davies – Luke's dad.'

'Oh!' She sounded taken aback.

'I'm sorry to disturb you, I hope you're not busy.'

'No. No, I'm just – bit of an essay crisis.' A nervous giggle.

'Oh dear.' He couldn't think of anything else to say, so he came straight to the point. 'Look, it's just – something funny's happened with Luke's Facebook profile, and I'm such an old fuddy-duddy when it comes to this sort of thing, and I wondered if you might be able to help explain it.'

'OK.' She sounded dubious.

'You see this photo has come up, and it says it's been posted from his account. You may have seen it.'

'No … I – I haven't looked at – I don't think I've checked Facebook today.'

He glanced down at her profile. There were several entries posted during the last twenty-four hours. But he understood what she was trying not to say, and he was grateful for it.

'Well, it's nothing really, I'm sure it's just a mistake. But I was wondering if he sometimes used, I don't know, other people's computers to look at Facebook. In case he'd left himself logged in, do you see?'

'Oh. Right. Yes. Um … I think so, probably. I mean we all use the computers in the library sometimes, even though we're not meant to.' She giggled. 'And sometimes, you know, if you're round at someone else's room and you're expecting a message or something.'

Absurdly, this little insight into his son's life made his eyes start to prickle. 'Yeah. Yeah, that's what I thought. Well, I'm sure that's what's happened. I expect whoever it was didn't even realise they were logged in as him until they put the photo up. It's just the one photo – they probably logged out as soon as they realised. Nothing to worry about.'

'I expect so. What a horrible shock for you, though!' She was a nice girl. Thoughtful.

'It was a bit.'

'What was it a photo of? It's just – you know, I might recognise the people in it.'

'Oh – well – nothing really. That's the funny thing. It's just a sort of black hole. I don't know why anyone would bother putting it up there.'

'How weird.' Her words made him suddenly conscious of how weird this conversation must be for her too, and he felt foolish for making such a fuss.

'I'd better let you go. Sorry to disturb you.'

'Don't worry!'

'Everything going alright with you?'

'Yeah. Well. You know. Essays!'

'Must be nearly the end of term, isn't it?'

'Next week. I can't wait to go home.'

He thought he managed to get the phone down before she could tell he was crying.

He made himself forget all about it. He even stopped checking Facebook every day, figuring it was time for him to move on like Luke's friends were obviously managing to. He started playing golf again. And he even said he'd go round to Mike and Eleanor's for Christmas Day because they wouldn't stop going on about it until he agreed.

And then this.

Luke Davies is cold. So cold.

He just kept staring at it.

15 December at 02:14
Comment/Like

A wave of anger rushed through him. Too right he would comment.

Richard Davies you sick bastard. How dare you?

How could anyone do this? The worst thing was that it must be someone who knew about Luke, who knew what had happened. That message wasn't the sort of thing you would put if you just stumbled across a stranger's Facebook still open on a random computer. It was deliberate. It was heartless. It was cruel.

Unless – unless. It *had* turned cold the night before. He had felt it when he got up for the loo in the middle of the night like he always had to these days, and the frost had been so heavy on his windscreen in the morning that clearing it off had made him late for work. Was there any way this could be the same thing he'd assumed had happened before – some poor innocent student stumbling into the library wanting to share the change in the weather with his friends, opening up Facebook and not noticing that it was still open under somebody else's name? Would that even be possible after all this time?

His finger hovered over the mouse. He looked at his son's smiling face, and his own face below it. Calling him a bastard. If he clicked Comment then it would be there for ever. It would be the first thing anyone saw on Luke's page. His own father, insulting his memory.

He deleted the words and clicked away from the page for good measure. He was going to have to get Luke's account closed down. That was the only thing for it.

He was up until four in the morning trying to work out how.

*

Richard Davies This is Luke's father. I do not know if someone has left the comment above on Luke's account by mistake. I hope so, because the alternative – that someone has been sick and cruel enough to write it as some kind of joke – is unthinkable. I have contacted

Facebook about having the comment removed. If it happens again I will have no choice but to get Luke's account permanently deleted.

16 December at 19:04

Several hours went past before there was any reply.

Luke Davies dad?
17 December at 05:12

*

The counsellor had told him there were four stages of grief he would have to work through before he started accepting Luke was gone. One of them was anger, and in a funny way it was good to have an excuse to give that full vent. He rang work and said he wouldn't be in until lunchtime. Instead he headed for the police station and refused to leave until he saw someone who would take his problem seriously. In the end he talked to a nice lady sergeant who was very sympathetic but pointed out that there wasn't a lot they could do unless the messages were actually threatening, and he had to admit that a picture of a black space and a few words, however upsetting, didn't really compare to some of the things that she mentioned.

He had even less luck with Facebook. It turned out to be impossible to speak to anyone real in charge of the website; instead he went round and round, clicking links to *Report a comment* and *Report a photo*, and getting drop-down menus which offered all sorts of reasons why something might be abusive or offensive, but none of them were *Someone is pretending to be my dead son*. He tried all the links for *Compromised accounts* because that seemed to fit the bill, but they turned out to be all about asking for money and things like spam and phishing which he didn't really understand but was pretty sure weren't what this was.

And then, while he was still online working his way through all this stuff – could they tell, he wondered – came the next message:

Luke Davies is lost
a few seconds ago

The policewoman had warned Richard that reacting could only encourage whoever it was, but he was so furious he couldn't help himself. He pulled up his son's profile and sent him a private message – he knew his way round the website by now, that was one thing to come out of all this.

Whoever you are and whatever your reason for doing this, just stop and let my son rest in peace. It is sick. I have been to the police about you.

He sat for a long time staring at the screen, but there was no reply.

As soon as he spotted it, he had no idea how he had missed it. He had spent so long staring at the stark black words on the page he had taken no notice of the grey text beneath it, save to note its inexorable march into the past: *about an hour ago; 2 hours ago; 3, 8, 19 hours ago; Monday at 00:13; 20 December at 00:13.* And he couldn't even swear the little symbol had been there all the time, because he had just assumed it was part of the website, one of the many little hieroglyphs littering Facebook that he didn't understand and didn't even notice any more.

But even he could tell what this one represented: it was a mobile phone.

Luke had one of the new mobiles: an iPhone 4 that Denise had bought him as a going-away present. He'd been so pleased with it. It wasn't with the rest of his stuff, which was still in the boxes in his room, or, rather, scattered all over the floor once Richard had been through them to make doubly sure. He tried ringing it, but he just got a message saying the phone was out of range.

If the messages were coming from Luke's phone, that meant someone had stolen it, which meant there had been a crime after all, which meant the police could do something.

His heart was pounding; he felt more alive than he had in weeks. He forced himself to sit down and think things through logically. Luke would have had his phone with him when he went windsurfing. Obviously he wouldn't have taken it out on the water because he'd never risk getting it damaged, so he must have left it with his clothes and stuff when he got changed into his wetsuit. So what had happened to it after the accident?

The first person he thought of was Sadie, but he quickly dismissed her; she hadn't been there when Luke died. And besides, he'd seen on Facebook a few days before that she had updated her relationship status with a little red heart next to some new boy's name, so he wasn't inclined to go running to her for help. Thinking about it, she had never even bothered to mention Luke using his phone to update Facebook when he had phoned specifically to ask her about that. Maybe someone didn't know his son quite as well as she liked to pretend to.

Instead he clicked through to the profile of the boy Alistair from the windsurfing club. He would know what had been done with Luke's stuff. Judging by his messages and the dozens of photographs he had posted in the past

31

few days – by mobile, he was spotting the symbol everywhere now – he was off skiing somewhere, but he had put his phone number on there like all the young ones did.

The dialling tone sounded foreign. He got the answering service, which wasn't all that surprising considering what time of night it was. In the end the message he left was so long and so complicated that it cut him off and he had to ring back to finish it.

While he was waiting, he logged on and left another message under his previous one:

> I know that you have my son's phone, and you should be aware that I have informed the police that it has been stolen and they are investigating. I would advise you to stop these heartless messages which can only increase the trouble you are going to find yourself in. And to take a long hard look at yourself.
> Luke's dad

*

'Richard Davies?'

'Yes?' He was so eager to take the call that he ignored the glares from everyone else in the meeting and ducked out into the corridor.

'This is Declan Thorne. You've been leaving messages on my son Alistair's mobile.'

'Yes. I wasn't sure if he was getting them, so I kept—'

'No, he received them. Listen, Mr Davies, I'm very sorry for your loss, but you must appreciate that your son's death was very upsetting for Alistair as well—'

'No, I know that. I'm not trying to – it's just …' He could hear himself gabbling, and forced himself to take a deep breath. 'I need to know what happened to Luke's possessions. The clothes he was wearing when he got changed to go out on the water, and the stuff he had with him. You see I've been getting these messages—'

'Alistair tells me that he passed everything that was in your son's locker on to his mother.'

'But did that include his iPhone? Because I think someone took it, you see.'

An icy pause. 'My son is not in the habit of stealing, Mr Davies. Especially not from those he considers friends.'

'No, I don't think it was him, of course, but could anyone else—'

'Now I'd appreciate it if you would leave us to enjoy our holiday in peace.'

He was dialling Denise's number the second the man put the phone down on him. The meeting could go on without him.

It took him all day to track her down. It turned out she had already gone to her sister's for Christmas. Elaine wasn't

33

best pleased when she picked up the phone to him. In fact she refused to let him speak to his ex-wife until he told her exactly what he wanted.

She was gone for a long time. He could hear carols playing in the background.

'Richard?' There weren't many tidings of comfort and joy in Denise's voice.

'Denise, I need to know what happened to Luke's phone. I know the boy from the windsurfing club gave you all the stuff that was in his locker, but was his phone there? It's just—'

She sounded bewildered, but mostly furious. 'We buried it with him, Richard. You know this.'

His head reeled. 'I … I didn't.'

'We discussed it at the undertaker's. How he was going to be in his best clothes, and have all his best stuff with him.'

He did vaguely remember something. Saying something about the watch they had bought Luke for his eighteenth.

'Is that all that you wanted?'

'Yes.'

She didn't bother to wish him a happy Christmas.

The phone you have dialled is out of range. The phone you have dialled is out of range. Every time he called the number the recorded woman told him the same thing.

But it was obviously still working for some things.

Dad please dont be angry
23 December at 23:56

im lost and im scared
Today at 01:32

Its so dark down here
Today at 02:26

Dad please my battery is going please come i cant find
the way out and its so cold
About an hour ago

The only light in the house was the cold grey glare of the computer screen. The only movement Richard had made in hours was to jog the mouse to revive the computer each time it dipped into darkness.

When he finally leaned forward it was all he could do to force his fingers to type.

Richard Davies where are you?

The answer came back within seconds.

I cant tell its so dark and I just keep going round

He bit his lip so hard that he could taste blood. His fingers drummed on the keyboard.

Richard Davies how do I know that you are my son?

The minutes ticked by.

When I was little you bought me the purple tellytubby for Christmas and I wouldn't stop crying because I wanted Dipsy

He felt like the walls were closing in on him. It was hard to breathe.

please dad please come im all on my own

He reached out with trembling fingers to find the off button on the side of the monitor and plunged the screen into blackness.

It would be several days before the police conceded to the increasingly noisy entreaties of the friends Richard Davies was supposed to be spending Christmas with to look into his disappearance, and well into the New Year before a uniformed constable bothered to come round to talk to his neighbours. They vaguely recalled seeing him packing his car on Christmas Eve and assumed he'd been going away to stay with family. Pushed a bit more, the husband admitted remembering being impressed by how well Richard seemed to be preparing for the journey: it was forecast to be the mildest December in years with no prospect of a white Christmas, but he'd been packing a shovel and blankets into the boot of his car.

It would be weeks before anyone thought to check Richard's Facebook account – and it never occurred to anyone to go back through his late son's, where they might have turned up such long-forgotten items as the questionnaire Luke had filled out and proudly displayed on his wall, which included the question: *What is your earliest childhood memory?*

By then Richard's own Facebook wall had long since tidied and rearranged itself, as they do according to their own mysterious algorithms when left untended for any length of time. But if anyone *had* bothered to look at it on the day after he was last seen, they would hardly have spotted anything out of the ordinary.

Bob Hardcastle fell asleep during the Queen!!! Is this treason????
25 December at 16:44

Bob Hardcastle phew! Now I understand why they call it stuffing!
25 December at 14:23

Sadie Barraclough is loving her presents!!!
25 December at 11:36

Guildford Golf Club season's greetings to all our members
25 December at 09:50

Bob Hardcastle merry xmas every1!
25 December at 07:47

Luke Davies is having a family reunion
25 December at 04:48

COME QUICK, DANGER

Fessenden, Reginald Aubrey *(1866–1932) Radio engineer
and inventor, born in East Bolton, Quebec, Canada. After
a varied career in industry and academic life as a teacher,
chemist, and electrical engineer, he became interested in
adapting wireless telegraphy for voice transmission. He
developed the principle of amplitude modulation (AM) and
made the first broadcast of speech and music on 24 Dec 1906
from Brant Rock, MA, which was heard over 500 miles away.*

CAMBRIDGE BIOGRAPHICAL ENCYCLOPAEDIA

NOT long after noon, when the sun is as high in the
sky as it will get today, and the squalls of the morning
have given way to an unrelieved flat greyness over Brant
Rock, she straps on her snowshoes and trudges the length
of Ocean Street carrying a tray of sandwiches for the fellows
in the laboratory. She has covered the plates with two nap-
kins fresh from the linen press that put the snow to shame,
and for once she is glad of one of Reginald's gadgets, the

vacuum flask he copied from an account of Dewar's original in *Scientific American*, for she has made a hot soup of winter squash and rosemary that will, she hopes, rid him of the tickle in the throat he was complaining of when he awoke. He will need his voice tonight, of all nights.

She can already hear the roar of the generator as she passes the chapel at the end of the village, each gravestone topped with a cap of freshly fallen snow. As she follows the shovelled path between the picket fences, the drifts on either side some three or four feet deep, the thump-whir-thump of the rotary transmitter adds its competing rhythm to the waves that crash on Blackman's Point below. She gazes up at the vast antenna which stabs up from the midst of the motley collection of buildings, expecting as ever to see some sign of the force that crackles within it, the energy that races up and down its spine – 750 times a second, her husband tells her – but, as ever, it stands impassive against the grey sky.

Inside, the transmitter's roar is loud enough to make conversation impossible. Her husband has his back to her, hunched over the alternator, his shoulders tense. Staines, in apron and goggles, raises a friendly hand as she sets the tray down on the table, holding up three fingers: *Hello; welcome; we'll be with you in three minutes.* She pulls up a stool, sits down to wait. After a while, she puts her mittened hands over her ears.

At last, at a signal from Reginald, Staines pulls the switch on the generator and the rotor ebbs and dies, the circle broken as its poles unblend and slow into individual visibility. Her husband turns, notices her for the first time, and his face breaks into a wide smile. Staines is already pulling off his gloves and tucking into the sandwiches.

'How will anyone hear you over that racket?' she asks, uncorking the vacuum flask.

'Oh, I won't be speaking from in here.' Her husband wipes his grease-stained fingers on a rag that looks no cleaner. 'We're rigging up a line to the old lookout station on the point.' He gestures to a thick cable wrapped with gutta-percha that runs across the laboratory's grimy floor and out through an open window on the building's seaward side. 'Arthur will be in here manning the transmitter, and I shall be out there, hunched over the microphone.'

'All alone?' she asks doubtfully.

He gives a grin. 'Oh no, my dear. I'll have the whole world in there with me.'

'Or at least those that are next to a telegraph receiver,' points out Staines through a mouthful of bread and potted meat.

'The modern world, then.' He accepts the cup she holds out for him and reaches for a sandwich.

She looks towards the open window and the roaring,

relentless ocean beyond. 'I pity any man stuck out there, tonight of all nights.'

He splutters crumbs into his beard in his enthusiasm. 'All the more reason to reach out to them: to let them share in the Christmas spirit. Do you not see, my dear, this is exactly what we are working for? Imagine: a few years from now, the farmer on his ranch, the cripple in his bed, the lighthouse keeper at his lonely watch, the young city clerk far from his family; all of them united in worship. One great universal congregation of the airwaves.'

She gives a weak smile. She's heard this speech before. 'Have you decided on your programme yet?'

'Oh yes.' He taps the violin case which lies upon the table. 'I thought I would start with a verse from a carol. And then something from the Gospels.'

'You must give them a warning first. They will be frightened out of their wits.'

He smiles. 'You think so?'

'To hear a human voice coming from their receiver, when all they are expecting is dots and dashes?'

He and Staines exchange amused glances. 'You think we will have a rash of sailors hurling themselves overboard in terror? Perhaps you're right. I shall begin by assuring them there is no need to be alarmed.'

Staines sings softly into his soup: '*Fear not, said he, for mighty dread had seized their troubled minds.*'

'You're quite right, Staines!' Reginald reaches for his Bible. 'That's just the thing: the warning to the shepherds. *Behold, I bring you good tidings of great joy, which shall be to all people.* The Gospel of Luke, isn't it?'

His assistant smiles at her reassuringly. 'Don't worry, Mrs Fessenden: we'll give them good warning.' He taps out the general alert on the table top – dah dit dah dit, dah dah dit dah – two times: CQ, CQ: Come Quick, Come Quick.

As if in answer, there comes a thumping on the door. She gives a little shriek, her hand to her throat. Ridiculous. It's just the mailman, doffing his hat and stamping the snow from his boots as her husband throws open the door for him.

'My dear fellow! Come in, come in. What brings you all the way out here in such weather?'

'Card for you, sir.' The man gazes around the laboratory, his eyes wide.

Her heart lifts. Is it from Kenny?

'West Orange, New Jersey,' her husband reads, and tears excitedly at the envelope. 'Ah! It must be from Edison.'

Of course. Why would Kenny write her here? He has the house address. She enclosed it with the package she sent to his barracks. She has heard nothing back.

Even in her disappointment she remembers her manners. 'Would you care to join us?' She gestures to the table. Even after Staines's best efforts, there are plenty

43

of sandwiches left. Her husband has hardly touched his own plate.

'No, thank you kindly, ma'am.' The man stands, turning his hat brim in his hands, staring up at the alien bulk of the spark gap transmitter and the alternator beside it.

'Oh, but you'll take something against the cold,' Reginald says distractedly, flipping open the card with its bright picture of Saint Nicholas on the front. 'Staines, fetch out the brandy.'

The mailman will accept a dram, if it's no trouble. Staines brings the bottle and four grubby glasses.

'*My dear Fezzie, I once told you that man had as much chance of broadcasting his voice as of jumping over the moon,*' her husband reads. '*I see from my almanac there will be no moon on Christmas Eve. Advise you take a good run-up.* Ha!' He shakes the letter at the startled mailman. 'You see that signature? Thom. Edison.'

'The electric man?'

'The very same.' He takes the glass that Staines is offering. 'I used to work for him. Your health.'

'Much obliged, sir.' The mailman sips his brandy, draws a brawny hand across his moustache, looks around the laboratory once more. 'And this is electricity, is it?' he ventures.

'Much more exciting,' Reginald assures him. 'This, my friend, is wireless telephony. Using this equipment, this very night, I intend to cast my own voice out across the

44

Atlantic. Every man with a wireless receiver will be able to hear me.'

She hates it when he shows off.

'You will put me out of business, sir.'

'Oh, not for many years yet. Come, would you like to look at it?'

He beckons him towards the transmitter, but the man holds back, unsure. 'Is it safe, sir? I would not like to hear voices in my head.'

Reginald chuckles in his superior way. 'My dear fellow, do you not realise that there are waves of sound passing around you at every moment? Through you, even.'

'You mean they are here, around me, invisible?'

'All around us there is a veritable cacophony of noise, if only we could hear it.' He throws an arm towards the ocean. 'Out there every boat captain and coastguard and weather bureau and shipping office is firing off messages into the aether, all squabbling and gossiping and arguing and feuding and calling out for help: a great maritime Babel spreading out across the waves courtesy of Messrs Morse and Marconi, and every dot and every dash of it is echoing off those cliffs below us and bouncing off the walls around us in the form of electromagnetic radiation each second that we stand here.'

The mailman gives a shudder. 'I do not like to think of that, sir. It does not seem right.'

Her husband roars with laughter and claps him on the shoulder in that bluff, gruff way he adopts with working men. The mailman puts down his glass and says he must be going.

'Shall I leave the rest of this food?' she asks, after the man has plodded back up the well-trodden path. Reginald has already returned to his instruments.

'Yes, yes, my dear. Prepare supper for the usual time – Arthur, you'll join us for a bite?'

She assures the assistant it will be no trouble. She took her holiday delivery from Hobson's the previous afternoon, and she has plenty laid in.

It has started to snow again as she walks back from the laboratory, and the tall antenna is singing in a sharp north wind that has blown up from Duxbury Bay. She cannot shake a feeling of anxiety that clings to her like sea mist. These are great forces that her husband is attempting to bend to his will. And for all his bombast, he does not fully understand them. Nobody can. And she cannot help but think that perhaps – though she knows how hard he would laugh at the idea – we are not meant to be their masters.

She fills her afternoon with baking, hauling tin after tin of shortbread and butter tarts from the oven even as she chops and boils the cranberries and grinds the herbs ready to dress tomorrow's goose. As the sun sinks behind

Green Harbor, she is whipping eggs and cream and sprin-
kling them with nutmeg and cinnamon ready for Reginald
to add the brandy when he returns. And all around her
the house creaks and sighs and whispers as she does her
rounds lighting the lamps. She does not want to be making
her Christmas preparations in this unfamiliar house, with
its bagged chandeliers and shuttered veranda, leased to
them cheaply because it is meant for summer lets. Her
life seems to have become a series of short-term leases,
following her husband's enthusiasms and the money he
needs to indulge them. She thinks back to the campus at
Allegheny, midnight mass and drinks with the Dean, and
the Provost reading out the grace at high table. Or their
home in Pittsburgh, with her mother's pianola tinkling
away in the drawing room, a roaring fire in the grate and
every room blazing, courtesy of Mr Westinghouse's Patent
Alternating Current Electric Lighting System. And she
thinks of Kenny far away in Texas, his first Christmas in
uniform, and she sends out a mother's silent prayer in the
hope that maybe it will transform itself into electromagnetic radiation and float out there across the dark land
to find him.

The men come in just after eight, blustering and stamping and complaining of a blizzard that has blown up 'out
of nowhere' – and, indeed, the world that is framed in
the doorway behind them is a maelstrom of black and

white. Between them they are carrying one of the receivers from the laboratory, which Reginald insists on setting up on the sideboard in the parlour, topping up the barretter with one of the bottles of sulphuric acid he keeps in the basement before he will even think about finishing off the nog. When both are ready – and he has joked about not getting the two bottles muddled, and she and Staines have dutifully laughed – she leads them through to the dining room where she has a tourtière waiting fresh from the stove and enough mashed potatoes and corn 'to see us through till 1907', as Reginald observes with a fondness she had almost forgotten.

But all too soon it is time for them to depart again, and that familiar feeling of unease descends on her shoulders once more. 'Could you not wait until morning?' she pleads as they pull on their coats and mufflers.

'Not if we wish to be heard.' Her husband shakes his head. 'Mr Armor has yet to receive a single one of our daylight transmissions at Machrihanish. He recorded the strongest signals close to midnight. The darkness is our friend.'

'I worry about you, out there alone.' She wrings a napkin in her hands.

'But Helen, my dear, I will not be alone.' He takes her in his arms. 'You will be with me.' He nods towards the receiver on the sideboard. 'Keep your finger on that switch and you will hear every word I utter, as clear as if I were in the next room. And so shall the rest of the world.'

His beard scratches against her cheek as he kisses her. And then he is gone, into the whirling night.

She sits in the cold parlour, listening to the ticking of the clock as it makes its way slowly towards the appointed hour. Out there in the darkness, other families sit round the table, exchange their gifts. Other mothers tuck excited children into bed with promises of magic in the morning, or huddle by the hearth and relish the tingling thrill of a fireside tale. She remembers her own grandmother, back in Quebec, pulling her close to tell her of how on Christmas Eve, at the stroke of midnight, when all good children are fast asleep, the beasts of the fields acquire the power of speech and talk among themselves, exchanging their masters' secrets. And how in the graveyards the dead themselves rise up and kneel at the foot of the cemetery cross to take communion from a golden-surpliced priest – the very same priest that used to minister to them before he too passed away – and when the mass has finished they all turn and give one last longing look towards the village before sighing and returning silently to their graves. And how anyone who slips out of their house to try to spy upon these strange events will be instantly struck dumb, or blind, or drop dead from fright where she stands, as God is her witness.

The clock strikes, startling her from her reverie. The wind is rattling the shutters on the veranda. She pulls her chair up to the sideboard, jams the headset to her ears, presses her finger to the receiver, and listens.

At first, all she hears is the sound of the storm, redoubled in ferocity and now inside her head, blowing and whining and shrieking. She closes her eyes, straining to make out any trace of her husband. And just as she thinks he has failed – that this is it, that dots and dashes will be the end of man's efforts to control the air around him – the chaos condenses into the heterodyne's whine and she hears a voice, so faintly.

… ssenden, speaking to you from Brant … ssachusetts. Do not be alarm …

And although she knows he is but a few hundred yards away from her, she also knows that if she can hear him, his voice can also be heard out there on Nantucket, and in Nova Scotia, and Newfoundland, and beyond, out in the measureless expanse of black ocean, in places unimaginably far away, mysterious names like Bailey, Rockall, Malin, Fastnet, Sole and Finisterre. And she has the sudden sense that right now, at this precise moment in time, the whole world is contracting in upon itself. And it is all because of her husband.

She can hear his violin sawing away now, marking out 'O Holy Night' through the storm of white noise that fills the earphones. Softly, she begins to sing along:

... A thrill of hope; the weary world rejoices,
For yonder breaks a new and glorious morn.
Fall on your knees! Oh, hear the angel voices!
O night divine, the night when Christ was born ...

And it was tonight, nineteen hundred and six years ago, that something else changed, something new came into the world and made everything different. And she knows, now, with a certainty far stronger than the wavering signal from the aerial on the point, which fizzles in and out of existence with every second, that her husband has succeeded. With this, now, he has changed the world.

His voice is coming clearer.

And suddenly there was with the angel a multitude of the heavenly host ... praising God, and saying ... to God in the highest, and on earth ... will toward men.

It ebbs and surges with the waves that roll relentlessly in from the Atlantic to spend themselves on the black rocks below.

And when they had seen ... made known abroad the saying which was told them ... And all they that heard it wondered at those things ... told them by the shepherds.

And she feels a great surge of pride in her breast for this man, this scruffy daydreamer she married sixteen long years ago when she was already carrying his child and has followed ever since from place to place, always on the move, one cart for their possessions and three for his equipment, never once staying long enough to put down roots and make a place their son could call home.

… but Mary kept all these things, and pondered them in her heart.

And now, after an aching pause that lasts long enough for her to think the transmission is over, or that through her own stupidity she has allowed the electrodes on her own receiver to slip out of sync or the barretter to run dry just as, in her carelessness, she has allowed the gas lamps to run down and dim, he speaks in his own voice. The man she loves.

… name is Reginald Aubrey Fessenden. I speak to you tonight from … boratory of the United States Weather Bureau in Brant Rock, Massachusetts … urge you, where'er you be, to write me on your return to shore … know that you are listening. For now, farew … Merry Christmas, one and all. I shall speak to you again by means … same apparatus on New Year's Eve … arewell. Farewell.

And as he bids the unseen listeners goodbye, the lamp on the table sputters and plunges the room into blackness. And another voice speaks out of the receiver. A cold, high, cruel voice.

Never see New Year

She starts back in the sudden darkness, but her finger does not leave the cold metal of the machine.

Never see morning

And it is gone, lost in the rush of noise that fills her headset as the transmitter runs down and returns the world to chaos. But she is not there to hear it. Tearing the phones from her ear she is gone, clattering through the unfamiliar rooms in the darkness with no time to put on snowshoes, hat or even a coat as she throws open the door and plunges out into the whirling cold outside.

The houses of Ocean Street are all but invisible. She keeps her head down, following the grey gash that has been cut through the snow down the middle of the highway, but it is more than twelve hours since the men attended to it with shovels and rock salt and it has frozen again, a thin sheet of treacherous ice beneath her indoor shoes. She slips and stumbles her way through the darkness, sobbing, tears of fear and frustration streaming down her cheeks and hitting the ground as ice. She cannot even see the great aerial ahead of her. There is no moon tonight.

As she passes the chapel at the end of the village she is aware of figures in the graveyard, movement among the headstones, a crowd that seems to mill toward the great stone cross capped with white, but all her fear is focused on the path ahead of her. The snow has obliterated the fences now, and out on the headland she is running through a world of white, a great field of lethal beauty. Her ankle twists beneath her and she falls, her arms breaking the faultless crust and plunging into sharp and painful

53

coldness. And she is screaming now, but there is no one to hear.

Just as she thinks she is sinking into coldness forever, ice filling her lungs and eyes and ears, and the snow sucking her down to wrap her in a wet and welcoming shroud, her numb hands close around something beneath the snow. A cable, wrapped in gutta-percha. She seizes it gratefully before she realises what it is. And then, with the new strength it gives her, she looks up and around her, and she sees the black bulk of the laboratory building to her right, behind her, and she realises how far she has strayed from the path. She can hear the pounding of the Atlantic somewhere below, dangerously close, and she sends up a silent prayer of thanks that she was stopped before she stumbled blindly over the cliffs and was dashed to pieces on the rocks below.

Forcing herself to be calm, she elbows herself up onto all fours, not daring to let go of the cable which is her only guide in this new world of whiteness. She hauls it up through the crust of the snow with the last reserves of strength she can find within herself. Its quivering bulk snakes off into darkness in both directions. One way, she knows, leads to the laboratory, and warmth, and safety. But her husband is at the other end, in the old lookout station right at the end of the point. And he is not alone.

Sobbing, half-frozen and demented with fear she pulls herself to her feet, and begins to force her way through deep, unbroken snow, following the cable, this gutta-percha lifeline, hand over hand, towards whatever is waiting for her.

The cork erupts from the bottle with a satisfying pop, and Staines brings it to the grubby glasses before it can bubble up, lest a drop be wasted.

'It's a bottle of Heidsieck I've had put aside since '99,' enthuses Fessenden. 'One of the finest from Allegheny's cellars. I feel we have earned it tonight.'

'Indeed, sir.' Staines passes him a glass and holds up his own. It is a shame the glasses are not a little less grubby, to be sure, but the pump has been frozen solid since mid-December, and he feels he has displayed inventiveness worthy of his title by plunging the tumblers into the drifts of snow outside the laboratory door to rinse them. God, it was bitter out there tonight. The wind from hell was blowing in off Duxbury Bay, and as it roared across the headland it made noises strange enough to strike fear into the heart of a more superstitious man than he. As he had paused outside the doorway it had sounded just like a woman screaming.

Fessenden clinks their glasses together. 'Well, Arthur, remember this moment.'

'I shall, sir.' He drinks. He is an ale man himself, but he will admit that this is rather fine.

'It very nearly didn't happen.'

'Indeed. I think we were right to abandon the old lookout station.'

Fessenden rolls the liquid round his mouth, smacks his lips. 'Indubitably. We could never have got a sufficient signal in this storm.'

'And your office worked very well in the event.'

'Yes.' The inventor smacks his hand upon the wooden partition above his desk. 'A little strengthening of this to make it soundproof before our next experiment, and we will have an ideal studio.'

They both drink deeply, pondering the future.

'Besides, the path was treacherous enough this after-noon when we laid the cable!' remarks Fessenden after a while. 'And in this blizzard? Imagine it. Impossible.'

'Indeed. I thought you were about to pitch over the precipice when we reached that turn.'

'And so I would, had I not abandoned the cable to save myself.'

'Do you think we will be able to retrieve it? It seems a shame to leave it dangling over the cliff like that.'

Fessenden shakes his head dismissively. 'We've plenty of cables. One will not be missed. It will be deep beneath the snow by now in any case. Perhaps we shall find it when the storm dies down.' He stretches and yawns. 'Let us wait and see what morning brings.'

THE OLD FOLK

SCHOOL finished early at lunchtime on the last day of term, but no one had told Mrs Wilson, the peripatetic music teacher, and since she had struggled all the way over on the ferry, Ishbel felt she really ought to go to her flute lesson as usual. 'I do feel terrible, keeping you from your holidays,' her teacher fretted while she split her instrument and tucked the pieces away neatly into their case. 'But I never know how many times I'll be able to make the crossing in January and February with the winter storms, and I'd hate you to fall behind.'

It meant that by the time Ishbel got to the school hall there was only one parcel for the old folks left, with the headmistress standing next to it seeming more than a little put out.

'Ah, there you are,' she said distractedly as she stuffed the marking she had been getting on with into her tapestry bag. 'I was worried you weren't coming.'

'No, I had a flute lesson,' Ishbel said apologetically, adding as a sweetener, 'I'm trying to keep up as many activities as I can for my UCAS form.'

'Mm, well, yes,' muttered the headmistress, not meeting her eye. She was searching through her bag for her car keys. Ishbel crossed to the table that had been set up in the middle of the room to look at the address scrawled on the outside of the cardboard box. Her heart sank. It was for the lone cottage right at the end of the Black Loch, one of the most remote on the island. She should have skipped her lesson after all.

'You'd better get moving, or you won't make it while the light lasts,' the headmistress said as she shouldered her bag. She obviously couldn't wait to get away from the school herself.

'It's alright, I've lights on my bike,' said Ishbel, lifting the box and shifting it to rest on her outstretched forearms. It wasn't too heavy.

'Oh, you're going on your bike?' The headmistress paused, biting her lip. 'Will you be able to manage that box?' She discreetly tucked away her own car keys as she spoke.

'It'll be fine. I've got a basket.'

'You won't be able to manage your instrument as well, though,' said the headmistress briskly, unhooking the flute case from Ishbel's shoulder and setting it down on the now empty table. 'Better to leave it here. It'll come to no harm. I'm locking up as I go.'

'What about practice?' asked Ishbel, but she was being bustled to the door and waved on as the headmistress locked up behind her. Never mind. The caretaker would probably be around tomorrow, and Ishbel reckoned she could charm him into letting her in to collect it. And if not, it wasn't as if she was going to get much practice done over the holidays anyway. Not with what she had planned.

The air that hit her as she walked out of the school was crisp and sharp, but not overwhelming. She was going to have to do that irritating compromise with her scarf as she cycled, ensuring her throat wasn't numbed as she panted up the hills but enduring a steamy neck and sweat trickling down her back and cleavage. And her maroon winter coat was far too warm to wear for cycling at all, but too warm not to wear when she was doing anything else. First world problems, she reminded herself as she dumped the charity box on top of her bike's wicker basket. But she was already looking forward to a good hot soak in the tub when she got home after this: an hour-long bath was her traditional start to the Christmas holidays. The rest of her family weren't so keen on the custom. There was just the one loo in the house.

The box, annoyingly, was too bulky and awkward to sit tight in the bike's oval basket, and she realised she was going to have to cycle with a balancing hand on it whenever she went round corners or up hills. She briefly tugged it open – the flaps had just been tucked into one another – to see if she could get away with rearranging its contents in the basket itself, but the thought of handing them over one by one seemed measly. These few cans and packets might be the only thing the poor old lady got to unwrap this year.

Instead, she shoved the box as firmly down into the basket as it would go – one of the sides crumpled a bit, but she could push that back out again before handing it over – and pedalled out through the school gates, pleased to find it balanced fine so long as she remembered what she was doing. There was only one car left in the car park. Ishbel had a feeling the headmistress was watching from inside to make sure she had left before she drove away herself, and wondered if she was planning to take the long way home to avoid overtaking or would just pretend not to see her.

She followed the north road out of the town. The school, a 1980s replacement for the Academy that still stood on the High Street but had long since been turned into the tourist office and library, was on the outskirts, so the few straggling bungalows were soon behind her and she was out in open countryside, rolling moorland on either side of the one-track road and no one to be seen but the odd sheep hunkered down on a verge or in the meagre shelter offered by the few rocks that broke the surface of the grass. She could hear nothing but the sound of the wind, which had already turned the right side of her face to ice, and the calls of the hooded crows she occasionally saw hopping about in the heather and squabbling over the few scraps they could salvage in these depths of the year.

The sky was still bright, or at least white. She'd started off full of confidence that she could make her delivery and be back before dark, but as her thighs started to burn as she struggled up the first hill on the route she realised she'd been overambitious. With a start she remembered this must be the shortest day.

Still, as she'd told the headmistress, she had her lights, and there was very little traffic on the north road, which led only to a few scattered farms – and, of course, Black Loch Cottage. Her mother worried about drunk drivers at this time of year, but she could see for miles on most of the route, and would easily be able to pull over onto the verge if she saw headlights coming.

It was satisfying to reach the peak and pause at a spot she still couldn't help thinking of as the top of the world. The moors stretched off to the east, rolling down to the jagged coastline where she could just make out white rollers breaking and fizzing onto the barely paler beach. To the west, the land stopped even more abruptly, ragged barbed wire marking the point beyond which only sheep and suicides should venture, and then there was a great nothingness all the way down to where the vastness of the Atlantic filled the distance. The shapes the teeming currents drew on its surface never ceased to amaze her; it was as if half a dozen oceans met and were tangling in an endless battle around the island's shores. Her grandmother used to say that on a clear summer's day you could stand here and gaze on four kingdoms, but that only worked if you let the Kingdom of Heaven be one of them, which Ishbel always felt was cheating. Today the haze of winter dampness meant nowhere at all was visible beyond the waves. The island stood alone.

She shook off such gloomy thoughts – she missed her granny at Christmas most of all – in favour of a more thrilling form of nostalgia as, steadying the box in the basket, she began to freewheel down the other side of the hill. She and her sisters had done this a million times when they were little, hurtling down at what felt like light speed, screeches of part terror, part joy trailing out behind them all the way. Sometimes they dared any tourist children who were staying on the island to join in, jeering and cajoling until they either gave in or sloped off, sobbing, back to their families. Only once had it ended in disaster, when a boy – she didn't think she had ever known his name, but he had an English accent – came off at the turn at the bottom where the road twisted to skirt the dark plantation tucked into the foot of the valley. He had ripped an impressive amount of skin from his legs when they got down to him, but insisted he was OK to walk back up even though he quite obviously wasn't. 'You can cry if you want to,' Ishbel remembered assuring him helpfully. He turned out – when one of his friends had been sent to fetch his dad from the caravan site – to have broken his kneecap. Ishbel and her sisters felt a bit guilty, but mostly disappointed that he didn't need the helicopter ambulance to come flying over but was just taken away on the regular ferry.

Afterwards she wasn't sure which came first: this memory surfacing in her mind or registering the icy patch where the trees threw such long shadows on the road at this time of year that daylight never touched it. All was confusion for a moment. She squeezed instinctively at the handlebars, but she was using one hand to steady the box so only one brake, thankfully the back one, locked on. The bike skidded, the box began to topple, she stretched out a leg to try to stop herself from tumbling and felt her ankle twist and the cold black surface of the road coming up to meet her.

She took the worst of the blow on her right leg and shoulder. It was lucky she had abandoned her flute: its box was flimsy and the instrument, which belonged to the school, might have been expensively damaged. How lucky only she was, she thought grumpily as she pushed herself up into a sitting position. Her shoulder and the top of her arm hurt, although her winter coat had cushioned the worst of the blow. Her thick woollen tights – uniform ones that she wasn't obliged to wear in the sixth form, but by god they were good for keeping the cold out – hadn't done quite as effective a job. The right leg was torn and laddered from ankle to knee, revealing skin that was bleeding quite badly and pitted with black grit and dirt. It hurt like fury.

'Bollocks,' she let herself shriek into the empty air. The road felt cold and damp on her bottom despite the thickness of her coat, but she didn't feel quite up to standing yet. Instead she satisfied herself with a few more yelled expletives. What was the point of being in the middle of nowhere if you couldn't swear at the top of your lungs?

She disturbed something in the plantation, and peered round to squint into the darkness between its neatly serried rows of trees to try to see what it was. The spruces, so pillared and separate at their bases, netted their higher branches together so thoroughly that neither light nor rain could penetrate, and she could see only a few dozen yards into the interior. As kids they had always been intrigued by the dry softness of the forest floor, creeping just inside its perimeter to run their fingers through the carpet of soft brown needles and point out to each other the alarming fungi that spurted among the roots or jutted from the trunks like steps for climbing. She had heard her father say the plantation was filled with alien species, and although she knew now he meant the Scandinavian spruces that the Forestry Commission had imported as the only trees capable of withstanding the conditions on the island, as a kid she was convinced it was these freakish growths that had somehow descended from outer space to take up residence there.

She couldn't see what it was that was moving. She thought she could still hear a muted rustling and cracking somewhere in there, but it was probably just a deer, or even a bird. It had given her quite a start, but no doubt it was more frightened of her than she ought to be of it.

Although ... another memory came swimming to the front of her mind, of another summer bike outing, when she and her screaming sisters had had to pedal for dear life to get away from a great black dog that erupted from nowhere and chased them down this road, its hot breath, it felt, right on their heels. That was years ago, though. The dog was probably dead by now, and it had almost certainly been a visitor anyway. No islander would be stupid enough to leave a dog roaming loose with sheep grazing. Anyway, that hadn't been here. Come to think of it, it had been further down the road, by the Black Loch, where she was headed now. They had actually dared each other to cycle as far as what someone had told them – or they might have told each other, she couldn't remember – was a witch's cottage. She suspected they might even have been planning to go up and knock on the door and run away. Nasty, she scolded herself now. Anyway, they never made it. The dog intervened and scared them so badly they had never cycled so far down the road again. And hopefully her charitable mission today would make up for their cruel intentions then.

Although it wasn't going to be quite as nice a gesture as she had intended, given that her crash had burst the box open and scattered its contents all over the road. She hauled herself to her feet, giving her leg a perfunctory brush down and looking forward to her hot bath even more, and began to gather the stuff together. A packet of Angel Delight had flopped into a puddle and was probably beyond rescuing, and a couple of the tins – one beans, one soup – had been dented out of shape. She pocketed the pudding and packed the tins back into the box, hemmed in by things that had survived better. They would still taste the same, she assured herself. Only as she rotated the bean tin so the kink in its side was less obvious did she suddenly notice that the best before date stamped on its top was the previous year. Her heart sank. How horrible. Everyone at the school had been asked to donate for the Old Folk's collection, and she and her mum had gone out and bought stuff specially. Someone had obviously just emptied out their cupboards of everything that was stale and out of date, figuring that poor pensioners should be grateful for it. How out of order was that?

She thought she had better check the rest of the contents, too. To her horror, the diabetic jam and the pasta sauce were well past their dates too. One of the tins of tomatoes had a best before from nearly three years ago. It was awful!

For a moment she thought about calling her mum, and asking her to take the car out to the Co-op and pick up a whole new selection – she would pay for it herself out of her Christmas money – but you couldn't get a phone signal at this end of the island, and besides, her mum had sounded quite crotchety that morning when she had tentatively raised the prospect of a lift, telling Ishbel that she had all manner of Christmas preparations to be getting on with and she was sixteen now and shouldn't take things on if she wasn't prepared to see them through. She had been in a foul mood that morning, although she obviously felt guilty about it, because when Ishbel called from the front door to say she was leaving for school her mother came rushing through from the kitchen and wrapped her in a bear hug, kissing her hair and muttering, 'Goodbye love, I'm sorry,' over and over again. And when she pulled away, she actually had tears in her eyes. She'd been funny like this a lot lately. Ishbel wondered if it was the menopause.

She supposed she could head back into town herself and buy new stuff, but that would probably take an hour or more, and the old woman had presumably been told to expect her that afternoon. She might not like opening her door to strangers after dark. Ishbel's granny never had, putting the chain on at dusk and telling anyone who would listen that 'nothing Godly ever crossed a threshold after sundown'. No, there was nothing for it but to press on and make her apologies when she got there. Does stuff in tins really go off anyway? She couldn't really see how it could. It would probably be OK.

She set off again, wobbling unsteadily on a bike she no longer totally trusted. She couldn't help casting sidelong glances into the plantation as she pedalled along. She had always enjoyed the optical illusion where the long avenues between the trees rearranged themselves into different formations as you passed, flipping from organic chaos to regimented straightness and back again. Now, though, all she had eyes for was brief glimpses of what might or might not be movement following her through the shadows.

Her right leg smarted every time she pushed down on the pedal. She looked down and saw that the blood was still flowing and had started to blot across her tights. That was all she needed. She had shaved and plucked and taken every other possible precaution to look good for Billy on their first time together, and now she was going to have to ruin the moment when she stripped off by revealing a great gash in her leg. She supposed for a moment she could keep her leggings on and roll them down, but dismissed the thought. That wasn't the sort of scene she had in mind at all. She wanted everything to be perfect.

They planned to head over to the mainland on the day after Boxing Day under the excuse of shopping in the sales. Billy had booked them a hotel. It was only one of the budget ones, but he'd been able to do it online, and they were both prepared to face down any funny looks they got in reception. They couldn't say anything anyway. Billy was seventeen, and he looked even older now he had stopped trying to grow a beard. And what they were doing was perfectly legal. (Actually, Billy's friend Jamie said that some of those hotels had an automated check-in, which is what they were secretly hoping for to save any embarrassment.) They had decided to buy the condoms on the mainland too. You could supposedly get them from the nurse in school if you made an appointment, and there was Boots on the High Street too, obviously, but both of those carried too much chance of gossip. It was a very small island.

She lost herself in thoughts of Billy as the trees receded behind her and she struggled up the second hill, thankfully not quite as steep as the first. Of how he had looked in his board shorts that summer, when they had spent day after day on the beach. Of the way his nipples hardened and stood out like little pink cake decorations when he came out of the water, and when she had pointed it out he had laughed and demanded to know, only half jokingly, if hers did the same, and she had shown him. Of the eighteenth birthday party on one of the farms where they had slipped off into a barn for more than an hour and it had felt like they might actually – but then they had been interrupted by his idiot friend Neville stumbling in and throwing up everywhere.

She'd been going to keep their plan a secret, but in the end she couldn't help confiding in her mum. They'd always been close, and it felt right to (although obviously she spared her the gory details). Mum had gone quiet for a bit, and dabbed at her eyes, and then given her a hug and said she was just being silly and she always knew this day would come but she could hardly believe her little girl had grown up so fast. That night when Dad came in from the fields, Mum shut herself up in the lounge with him, which was a bit alarming, but when Ishbel came down from doing her homework he just grunted at her over the top of his mug of tea and didn't say anything, although she thought she had caught him looking at her in a funny way a few times in the days that followed. Still, she translated this as her parents signalling, if not quite their approval, their acceptance of what was going to happen, although she thought it might be pushing it to put some sexy new underwear on her Christmas list. She might have to actually go to the sales on the mainland for that. And if it was too expensive, she had spent plenty of time working out what matching bits she already had that would do.

She reached the summit and caught her first glimpse of her destination, the tiny cottage a grey mark on the far bank of the loch that filled the bowl of the valley beneath her. The hills to the west rose high, their long shadows falling right across the water's surface. It was thick peat that darkened the Black Loch and gave it its name, but the low winter sun rendered it literal. Not a reed broke the water's surface, barely a ripple disturbed it; it lay like a dark mirror reflecting an impassive sky. Ishbel shivered, and not just from the cold wind that had sought her out again as she crested the peak. She had remembered something else her granny had liked to say: that the reason no fish swam in the Black Loch, and no child ever should either, was that it had no bottom and went 'all the way down to hell and the de'il'.

She knew that really it was just a clever old woman's way of keeping them safely away from deep water – if she'd issued a flat-out ban, they'd have been on the banks in their cozzies within the day – but right now, with the sun sinking colourlessly behind the hills and the darkness seeming to ooze out beyond the loch's banks and spread inkily over the surrounding landscape, it felt all too easy to believe.

She shook the thought from her head and, more cautious on this descent, rode on down to the water's edge, keeping her gaze focused on the cottage, which was already beginning to fade into the encroaching gloom. It stopped her from turning to look at the road behind her and check it was definitely empty, an impulse she had been fighting for quite some time now.

The wind had vanished now that she was down in the valley. There were no birds any more, either. All she could hear was the lapping of the water at the edge of the loch, tiny waves throwing themselves out at the narrow shore only to be endlessly sucked back into the black depths.

She paused for a moment to switch her bike lights on, for comfort as much as for safety. Maybe the old lady would be looking out of her window and see them as she wobbled towards her, and know she had not been forgotten. Ishbel began to picture her throwing open the door delightedly and inviting her in for a warming drink at her fireside to fortify her against her journey home; in her fantasy her hostess had the face of her own grandmother. She knew it was hardly likely. The whole point of this exercise was to help those who had barely enough food for themselves. If she was offered as much as a cup of tea, she was probably morally obliged to turn it down. And besides, she could see enough of the cottage to make out that there were no lights on, or smoke coming from the chimney. The poor woman might not even be able to afford to switch her heating on.

Imagine living out here, beyond the edge of everything. Doubly removed, as if the island was not isolation enough. An exile within an exile. Ishbel loved the island in the fierce way that all those born there had to, loved it at least by long summer daylight when a constant stream of visitors arrived to remind you anew of its beauties and bring with them reassurance that there was a real world out there beyond its shores. But she felt just as strongly within herself that her future lay on the mainland. For as long as she could remember, every picture she had of her grown-up self – an Ishbel with longer and mysteriously straighter hair, who wore less-is-more make-up and clothes that weren't compromise buys from the few online places that offered off-shore delivery – was as a resident of the mainland, with all the comforts and opportunities those born there took for granted. But it was a truth she hadn't spoken out loud until the parents' evening that term. That was when the headmistress sat her mum and dad down to talk through her higher education options and started pulling out leaflets for remote learning modules. Plucking up her courage, Ishbel had interrupted the adults' cosy exchange about the marvellous things technology had made possible these days to say no, she wanted to apply to universities on the mainland and she had even researched which course. She would never forget the dismay on her dad's face, though she was surprised to see the headmistress giving her the same look.

Of course, Ishbel knew why. She had heard all the worried talk over the years about how the island would die if its young folk kept moving away. But she had watched it happen, too – Suzie McAllister, in the year above her, so glamorous with her hockey-player's legs, and Bridie McAllan the year before, head girl but gone before the school year was even out, never to return for as much as a visit – and if anything, the island was thriving. Life went on in the same old ways. There were still fish in the sea, and sheep on the moors, and kids being born and filing their way through the gates of the primary school each September, just as sure as spring came around and the flowers bloomed on the machair year after year. In fact, life was a thousand times better than in her grandmother's day, when winter storms would cut the island off for months at a time, the boats hauled up uselessly above the tideline and rats in the stores and children taking sick and wasting away in the cold and the darkness.

But with her grandmother gone, no one seemed to speak of those days any more. Just as, for all their fears for the future, no one ever seemed to mention the girls that had gone.

She had arrived at the end of the water. The cottage was ahead of her, barely there in the gloom. A Rorschach blot of once-white wall was all that showed through a mess of dark ivy clutching both garden and house in a choking grasp. No lights burned in the windows. It looked as if no one was living there. It looked as if no one living had been there for a very long time.

Ishbel dismounted onto legs that were trembling not just from the exertion of the ride. She leaned her bike against a mass of greenery from which a few rusty spikes of railing protruded like ribs, twisting its handlebars so that her front lamp would light her way up the mossy path to the front door. All she could hear was the lapping of the water at the edge of the loch. She slid the Christmas offering from its basket.

It was only as she reached the door and stretched out a gloved hand to rap on its peeling surface that she glanced down at the writing on the box and realised the address had no name with it. She didn't know who she was meant to be delivering to. She had no idea who might be waiting inside.

The morning after the winter solstice was clear and bright, but the headmistress had lived on the island all her life and knew that blue skies could be fleeting and you must grab a chance to use the sunlight when you get it. She roused her husband and the two of them were away out of the house before any of their grandchildren had woken.

They drove in silence, seeing few people, and fewer people chose to see them. The town's two constables, parked up in their panda car near the school on an early patrol, gave them a nod of acknowledgement as they passed, but quickly looked away. Part way up the north road, just before the plantation, they had to pull over to allow a tractor to pass, and although the driver, whose family had been farming on the island for ten generations, raised a hand in thanks, he was careful not to meet their eyes.

Outside the cottage they realised they should have put down the back seats of the Volvo ready for Ishbel's bike, and there was a brief row in hushed voices. The headmistress left her husband hurriedly sorting it out while she scurried up the path, her eyes sweeping from side to side, carefully not glancing up at the door of the building. She spotted the cardboard box half-hidden in the greenery to the right of the step. The ivy looked as if it had already made a start on smothering it.

Once they were safely back on the other side of the loch and speeding back towards the town, the bike rattling in the back as the front light spilled the last of its battery power uselessly up at the car's roof, the headmistress peeled back the soggy cardboard and did a quick inventory of the box's contents. A couple of the tins had somehow got battered out of shape and would have to be replaced. And the box itself was clearly beyond further use. But everything else would do for at least another year.

PANIC ROOM

Your first thought, not even a thought but a certain knowledge that hits you like a lead weight before you are fully awake: it is happening again.

Your second thought, brain kicking in and beginning to process the event before your eyes have even had time to open: how can it be happening again?

Then there are no more thoughts, not even time to breathe, only instinct and muscle memory as you wrench yourself from sleep and reach out for Mia, who, thank G-d, is beside you, as you have always kept her beside you ever since that first terrible night. And you scoop her up, one arm beneath her rounded shoulders and one wrapping the trails of her nightdress tightly around her little legs, and carry her – there is no weight to her, although you know in this moment that you could lift tons, wrench aside boulders or lift cars if that was what it would take to make your child safe – across the room in just two or three strides, *the strides of an Amazon, hoisting her up to your shoulder and holding her one-handed so the other is free to reach out and SLAM on the magic patch on the wall. And for a moment that part of you that is silently screaming inside is saying, what if it doesn't work what if after all this practice all these dummy runs all these false alarms it does not open up, but the great dark gap is yawning open before you can even pull back your hand and then you are through on the other side and it is closed and the wall is solid behind you and you are both safe.*

And it is only then, once the pair of you are locked away tight at the very heart of the house, where no one can ever reach you, that you allow yourself to make any noise, a low moan of anguish mixed with relief.

And Mia speaks too, her voice tiny, a confused whisper directly into your ear.

'What's happening, Mama?'

'Ssh. Ssh. We're safe, it's OK. It's happening again, there are people in the house, but we are safe in here.'

She pulls away to look you directly in the face, her eyes wide and terrified. 'Again?'

'Ssh,' you tell her again, stroking those beautiful curls, trying to pass on the reassurance you so badly need yourself. 'We're safe this time. Safe in here. I promise.'

And her face crumples, folds in on itself as the tears begin to flow. 'I miss Dada!'

And all you can do is cuddle her close, running your fingers through her hair, trying to share out some warmth between you. 'I know, honey, I know. I do too. I wish he could be here with us, but I promise you, I am here, and this time I will keep you safe.'

But her bitter sobs go on, jagged and gasping, and there is nothing you can do but hold her close and shush her because you need to listen, even through the thickness of these walls you need to hear who these people are, why they are here in your house, why they have come back. The noise came from downstairs. They aren't even making any effort to hide it. Brazenly bursting in through the front door, in full sight of the whole street. And you can only hope that someone was up to see it, that this time one of the neighbours might have caught a glimpse of them, and have raised the alarm. That's what they promised you before you moved in. 'Everyone looks out for each other round here.'

'It's a real close-knit community round here, the kind you don't find so much these days. Everyone looking out for each other, but not too in your face, you know what I mean? Next door there's a very sweet older couple, retired, you couldn't ask for nicer neighbours. And the folks on the other side, I met the lady this morning and she's real nice too. She's expecting a baby, any day now. She's hee-uge.' The realtor gestured for them to precede her into the house. 'You got a family of your own?'

'Just one,' the woman confirmed with a shy smile as she stepped past her into the hallway. 'A daughter. She's at preschool right now.'

'Well, just you let me know if you need to arrange a second viewing so she can come check the place out herself. I'm here till six,' the realtor assured her with a beaming smile. 'The choice of schools around here is fantastic, you should have all the details in the file, yeah?'

The man nodded and smiled, tapping the glossy folder under his arm. 'It's part of the reason we're looking in this area.'

'Well of course. I gotta say, there is a real family feel to this whole neighbourhood. A real good vibe.'

Except when it mattered. That night when the men came, the blinds stayed closed, the lights off. The old couple next door took out their hearing aids at bedtime. The fractious baby on the other side slept right through the night for once, and let his exhausted parents do the same. No one heard a thing. No one came to help.

And you know in your cold heart that no one will come this time, either. And Benjamin, who would once have done everything in his power to protect the pair of you, cannot do anything this time, because your husband, the love of your life, the man you thought you would be with forever – he is gone.

You and Mia are on your own.

The realtor pushed the front door to as gently as she could. She had tacked the ostentatious wreath up on the outside herself not half an hour ago, and she didn't entirely trust it to hold. To draw attention away, she pointed a lacquered fingernail downwards. 'Now, I would just ask you to take a moment to appreciate these floors, they are solid hardwood and they go right the way through to the kitchen in the back. They've all been resanded and polished throughout, just very recently.'

'Oh!' the woman laughed nervously. 'Should we take off our shoes?'

'Don't you worry, honey.' The realtor laid a hand on her arm, keeping it there precisely the well-practised amount of time to be friendly, and not long enough to be weird. She had a pack of wet wipes in her bag: she would get down on her hands and knees and remove any scuff marks before the next clients were due. And she could always rearrange the rugs. She brought those with her as well.

The wall is hopeless. Too solid now it is closed up, too sound-proof to hear anything from this distance. So you ease Mia down and, shushing her once more, you drop, and, sweeping your hair back over your shoulder and holding it there with one shaking hand, press your ear to the bare floor. Yes, they are downstairs. Two of them at least, maybe more. You can make out voices, but more than that, the sound of clumping footsteps. They are making no effort to be quiet. Oh no. They want you to know they are here.

Mia is whimpering. You sit up again and pull her close. 'Don't worry, my love, they can't get to us in here. We're safe. We have everything we need here. We can stay forever if we need to.'

She sniffles. 'But Dada!'

The thought of Benjamin cuts through you like ice. 'I know, baby, but that won't happen to us, I promise. It's different now. We have this place. All we have to do is sit tight. And they will go away. I promise you. Once they realise we are in here and there is nothing they can do to get us out, they will go away.'

You gently lift her head until she is looking straight into your eyes. 'I will protect you. Do you believe me?'

And Mia nods, as bravely as she can. And you hope it is only in your head, and not hers, that a little voice is saying, 'That's what he promised, too.'

And your mind goes back to that day when you and Benjamin first set eyes upon this place. You had never felt so certain of your togetherness as when you both knew in the same instant that the end had come to your search for your forever home.

*

'Come on through into the living area. Open plan, as you can see. And the view from this picture window. Isn't it to die for?'

'Oh wow!' the wife gasped. In truth, the view was exactly what you would expect, of the street outside, framed by the trees still holding the last of their yellow and orange leaves. But it was a very nice street. As her husband had pointed out as they were parking up, it ought to be at this price.

'All open plan,' the realtor confirmed, still on the move. 'The fireplace I love. The Residents' Association have very strict rules on fossil fuels, as you might hope with a little one of your own, but as a feature piece, I gotta say it is just stunning.' Before they knew it, she had swept them on through and was taking up a stance beside the vast kitchen island and the platter of citrus fruits she had artfully arranged there. 'Perfect for entertaining, or just for quiet family dinners. And it comes with all the facilities, all plumbed in, ready for use. Refrigerator, dishwasher, all brand new, you got all your laundry machines through there beyond the walk-in pantry.'

'Oh, gosh. It's real nice, isn't it?' The woman looked to her husband for approval, and he gave it with a smile. He was thinking about the cost. And he worried that the realtor realised that, so he overcompensated.

'It's all a real nice finish.' He grinned inanely.

'It's so funny you should say that,' beamed the realtor with surprising sincerity. 'Because those are just the words I used myself when I first came in here. A real nice finish. Fact is, the owner just had the whole place refurbished, freshly painted throughout, all done to the highest standard. If you wanted, you could just move in and start living here tomorrow, you wouldn't need to freshen up a thing.'

His wife re-emerged from the door on the far side of the room and they exchanged a look. 'It's perfect.'

You thought you would grow old here together. That Mia would grow up, go off to college, one day bring you back grandchildren who would slide up and down those polished floors in their socks, giggling as the two of you, white-haired, looked on indulgently from your recliners in that great front room. But it was not to be. Because he is gone. And he is never coming back. They took him from you.

And now they have come back. As you somehow always knew they would. You can hear them moving around downstairs. Checking every room. Searching them. But this time you, you and Mia, you are safe up here. No one can get you now. No one, ever. But you feel a chill spread through you nonetheless, as you hear their heavy footsteps begin to climb the stairs.

*

'But that's the beauty of a place like this: if you choose, you can do whatever you want with it,' said the realtor, gesturing expansively around. 'Take the arrangement of the rooms up here: currently you got your master bedroom and two smaller bedrooms. Now the master bedroom I am guessing you would want to leave alone – it's a great size, and it's got this exquisite wood panelling from the turn of the century.' She threw open the door to demonstrate, and the couple peered through and made the appreciative noises that were expected. Rather than go in, however, she lingered on the landing. 'All this out here, though, this is just drywall.' She curled her long nails into her fist – she was not going to risk chipping one, although if she managed to bring off this sale she would treat herself to a whole new set – and rapped hard upon the wall beside her. 'You could smash through and do whatever you wanted to do with them. Gut them completely if you wanted to.'

Feeling the need to demonstrate something – though he owned only the most rudimentary toolkit and tended to get someone in to do anything more complex than changing a light bulb – the husband stepped forward and delivered his own series of sharp raps on the wall, which echoed hollowly.

'I'm not sure we'd want …' said the wife, hesitantly.

'Maybe not now,' the realtor said. 'But it's the sort of thing you could take your time over. Be sure to get exactly what you want. In the future, if things change. You never know what's gonna happen!'

You can't help it. You do not want Mia to know anything of what you have just overheard, but the horror of it escapes you as a strangled gasp as you reel away from the wall.

'What happened, Mama?'

'Nothing!' you whisper shrilly, pulling her to you again and wrapping an arm around her head to block her ears, so she will never have to hear anything so awful. 'We just have to stay in here. Stay quiet.' Your voice, your tone, the tenseness in your body, all of them are telling her how terrified you are, even as you try to speak calmly. So you try to force a smile into your voice, and put it in terms a child – because Mia is still so young, so very young – can take in. 'As quiet as mice, the two of us. Mice in our mousehole.'

'But why are they banging on the wall?' she whimpers. 'Are they going to break in?'

'No, no, no,' you assure her. 'They can't get to us. I promise. There's no way they can get to us.'

And then the banging comes from much closer, and louder, and you know that they have found your hiding place.

*

The realtor sensed she was losing them. Not doer uppers, this pair: more nesters. And maybe they didn't want more kids, or couldn't have more for medical reasons, or maybe they were just the sort that like to draw their world close around them and keep things as they are. Cautious. The kind that like security. In which case she thought she had just the thing that would sell this place to them.

So now she did gesture them on into the master bedroom. She did not want them to linger too long in here, cold and unfurnished and far from its best as it was – although the emptiness did allow viewers to appreciate the woodwork, which did date, as she said, to the turn of the century, though not necessarily the one people might assume she was talking about. But before they could ask any questions, she strode straight over to the far side of the room. 'This, I gotta say, is a unique feature. None of the other houses in this street have one of these. Listen.' She reached out her fist again and rapped on the wall, which gave a pleasingly different sound. 'This wall here, this one, is going nowhere. There's three inches of solid steel behind this. Look.' She reached out to an electronic panel, halfway up the wall. 'Whaddya think this is?'

'A safe?' The husband hazarded a guess.

The realtor shook her head, her wide smile for the first time showing in her eyes as well. 'Kinda, I guess. Look.' She punched a combination into the keypad, and enjoyed the look on their faces as the panel beside it gaped open, a door into the blackness beyond. 'Your own panic room,' she said proudly. 'Impregnable. You could hole up in there for as long as you needed to, and no one would be able to get to you.'

Dammit, she was convinced this would be the selling point. But the wife – and if she'd learned anything, it was always the wife that made the decisions – was looking at her in wide-eyed horror.

'Why the hell would we need to?' she asked.

You can't help yourself. You stand up, and before you know it, you are banging your fists right back on this side of the wall, hammering away defiantly, because they know you are in here now and you have nothing to lose. You know exactly what their plan is now, maybe you knew it from the moment you awoke and heard them downstairs, but now you are certain, because you have heard what they said: they want to smash their way in and gut you both, to take their time over it, to get exactly what they want from you. And you will never, never allow that to happen. 'Get out!' you scream, again and again. 'Get out, get out, get out!'

'What was that noise?' asked the husband.

'Oh. You know these old houses. Creaking bones.' The realtor's smile was faltering now. She made a note to reapply her lipstick, maybe touch up her whole face, if she had time before the next viewing. Because she knew now, could feel that sense in her gut that had come with years of doing this job, that this one would not be the last viewing. She'd lost them.

Nevertheless, she persisted. 'Have a look inside,' she invited him. 'There's plenty of room in there for a whole family. All the supplies you might want to store in there too, food, fresh water. And once that door is shut behind you, there's no way it's opening again from the outside. No way on earth.'

He moved forward gingerly, poked his head inside, not wanting to commit his whole self. The wife stayed exactly where she was. She had got her phone out now. This was exactly what the realtor didn't want to happen.

'It all looks very new,' he said, for want of anything else to say.

'It is,' said the realtor dully. She was watching the wife stab away at her phone screen. 'The owner had it put in last year. After …'

'After?' The husband pulled his head back into the room.

'I knew it. David, look at this. I said there was some-thing wrong, why this place was going for so much less than the other places round here. Look!' The wife was holding up her phone triumphantly. The realtor could see what was on the screen: the *Post* story. That was the worst of all of them.

Her husband went scuttling across to her, embarrassed. 'Calm down, honey.'

'Don't tell me to calm down! This is the Liebermann Murder House!'

'You have got to be kidding me!' He looked at the realtor accusingly. She just shrugged and spread her hands. It had been a very long day.

'Where the mother and her little girl got killed!' his wife continued, a shrill edge to her voice. 'Last year, you remember!'

'I do, I do.'

The realtor had a headache now. The banging and the screaming from the walls weren't helping. Abandoning any hope of a sale now, she turned and put her lips just inches from the wood panelling, and shrieked, 'Would you please for once just shut the fuck up!'

When she turned back, the couple had already gone. She could hear their heavy footsteps clattering down the stairs, and she listened to them thump across the hallway and the front door slamming behind them.

They are going. We have won.

You pick up Mia – she weighs nothing, she is not even skin and bones – and clutch her to you. The two of you will never, ever let go of one another. And you will never, ever leave this place. For although you can pass within the walls at will – a neat trick, though cold comfort compared to what you have lost – you can never go beyond them. Just as your husband, Mia's father, your beloved Benjamin, who was away on that one night that could have made a difference, away at a surgical conference in New Jersey where he had to be awakened by hotel staff with the terrible, the worst of all news, has sworn that while he will spend whatever it takes to sell the place, he will never cross the threshold of this house again for as long as he lives.

Back downstairs, the realtor slumps onto one of the stools at the vast kitchen island. Real Calacatta marble. If it was anywhere else it would sell the house by itself. She pops a couple of Advil, and takes a long swig from the water bottle she has tidied away into one of the empty drawers beneath. It contains a good 50 centilitres of vodka, topped up (but not too much) with soda. It helps her get through the days.

She has fifteen minutes left before her next viewing is due. She usually waits outside on the stoop between appointments. It's easier that way. That's where she met and chatted to the next-door neighbour earlier, helped her down her own steps with her toddler's stroller, and asked the boy if he was looking forward to the arrival of his little brother or sister any day now.

But for once the house is actually quiet. So she may as well take the opportunity to return the voice message that has been sitting on her phone since earlier that afternoon.

'Hey there, Dr Liebermann. It's Sherelle, from Thomson Realty.' She was hoping to get his voicemail, not to have to speak to him direct. She knows the cops couldn't find any evidence of his involvement in the crime, despite all the stuff the papers dug up on him, but the sound of his voice still gives her a creepy feeling. To shake it off, she stands up and wanders through to the open-plan living room as she talks. 'We haven't had any bites as yet, but I'mma keep trying. I've still got a few appointments to get through this afternoon, and more scheduled for next week.'

She has reached the front room. She stretches out a Jimmy Choo – real ones, which she bought for herself with the commission she made when she finally managed to sell another haunted house down in Brooklyn Heights – and adjusts the positioning of one of the sheepskin rugs in front of the fireplace. She swears that, despite the sanding and the polishing, the bloodstains still show through.

THE HAWTHORN TREE

D OWNSIZING. That's what we told people. It was the quickest and easiest way to explain what we were doing. Because then it sounds like something admirable, it sounds like a lifestyle choice, like something they have programmes on Channel 4 about, rather than what it really was, which was something a lot messier and more confusing that I'm not sure either of us could have found the right words for even if we'd wanted to. 'Ooh, you are lucky,' more than one person told me. 'We dream of doing something like that.' I just smiled, and something about the way I smiled usually made them tell me how brave I was too.

But it didn't feel like downsizing. Not when we stood at the back door and looked at the vast expanse of green hill behind us, and beyond that the big sky. A proper sky, stretching all the way from east to west without a single building to block the view, and one that was filled with stars at night-time. I don't think the girls had ever seen the stars properly. You don't, living in London. I remember saying to Tom that it felt like we were living life on a whole different scale.

Of course it wasn't perfect. The survey said we would need a new roof sooner rather than later, and there were a couple of windows at the front that were rotten through and needed replacing straight away, but the estate agent put us on to a local builder who got them done before we even moved in and didn't charge that much more than we'd have expected to pay in town. And it was a shame the garden was north-facing. The hill that had seemed to cradle the cottage protectively when we came to view it in the summer turned out to overshadow it in the winter, blocking every scrap of sun from the raggedy back garden that trailed up its slope, but Tom was still convinced he could do something with it. There wasn't a scrap of vegetation growing on the windswept hillside above, just sheep-cropped wiry grass uninterrupted by so much as a gorse bush, but Tom insisted that there must have been a garden here in the past, and he could make one again.

I don't know where his confidence came from. It wasn't as if he'd ever done much in the way of gardening before, but somehow that was part and parcel of the new start.

He had such big ideas. When he hacked all the brambles back he found the original wall, a drystone one, all tumbled down and coated with moss, and he was convinced he was going to rebuild it, even though there didn't seem any point because there was nothing behind the garden but the hill and the worst thing that was likely to come in was surely a sheep or maybe a lost rambler. But he joined the local library with the girls and came back with a book about drystone walling to go with all the ones about growing vegetables. He did at least agree that it was a job to put off till next year, if he was going to stand a chance of getting any veg sewn in time for the spring. Although he was absolutely determined to get rid of the old hawthorn tree that stood at the very top of the garden, because he'd got it into his head it was shading the place where he wanted his rhubarb to go. I'd protested that it might get us into trouble with the local council – it was properly old, a great gnarled thing that looked like it had been there for hundreds of years – but once Tom sets his heart on something, there's no telling him. I tried to suggest we at least get a tree surgeon in to do a proper job of it, but he insisted he could do it himself, and he went out to the garden centre and came back with an axe so heavy and lethally sharp that it set me off worrying about exactly how long ambulance response times must be all the way out here.

At least it kept him busy. The idea was that he was going to pick up locum work while I commuted, but between the end of August when we moved in and the end of November I don't think he got more than four or five days in all. A lot of the surgeries he contacted said they were waiting for their budgets to be set under the new system and they might be able to give him more work in the new financial year, but that wasn't much use in the meantime. I know it got him down, but I didn't want to push it in case he took it as criticism. We were alright for a while, anyway. Our friends back in London couldn't believe it when we told them how little we'd paid for the cottage. It was the first time in our lives we hadn't had to worry about mortgage payments.

It also meant Tom was around while the girls were getting settled in their new school in the village, which I have to say they took to like ducks to water. Within days they seemed to have their little group of friends and invitations round to play. And soon they were arriving back from their friends' houses with new enthusiasms like riding lessons or keeping chickens that would never have crossed their minds in a million years if we'd stayed where we were. It was amazing to think they would grow up as countryside kids and would barely remember the years they spent living in the city.

I was finding the commute just about manageable, though having to get up ever earlier to de-ice the car in the mornings as the year wore on started to do my head in. Even then, though, being able to look up and see the sun just beginning to peek over the brow of the hill and set the frost on the peak shimmering – or just the pink glow in the fog that hung around the summit some mornings – well, it made it almost worthwhile. Thankfully Tom was happy to sort out the kids on the weekend mornings and let me lie in, then enjoy a long bath and a lazy few hours to myself. I always had grand plans for us to go on days out and long walks exploring the area, but somehow with the days drawing in we never quite managed it. We'd never even got as far as the top of the hill behind our house. A nice woman I bumped into at the village shop had told me it was an old fort and there were neolithic long barrows and standing stones up there, and that the views from the top were breathtaking. 'Don't worry,' Tom told me one Sunday night when I was moaning to him about how we weren't taking advantage of where we were for the girls' sake. 'We've got years to explore. We're not going anywhere.'

You see, that's the way we'd been talking. About the future. Not all the time, but regularly, whether it was his seed catalogues, or locum work picking up in the spring, or getting a dog, which was the girls' latest obsession. All things that meant he was planning to be around for a long time. That's what I couldn't convince the police about. Because of course once they'd found out about the affair, and the fact I'd given him two options – new start or final end – well, you could tell by their faces that they'd made their mind up exactly what had happened and there was no point them wasting their time looking for someone who didn't want to be found.

And I considered that too, don't get me wrong. I spent ages going over every conversation we'd had since we moved, any signs I might have missed that he was having second thoughts or that he'd made the wrong decision. I even phoned Her. That was probably a mistake, especially having drunk most of a bottle of wine to pluck up the courage, but it was clear from her voice that he hadn't been in touch with her and she didn't have any idea where he was. She kept saying, 'Missing? What do you mean missing?', as if there was any clearer way of explaining it. She even asked me to let her know if I had any news. I told her not to hold her breath.

I'm getting ahead of myself. It happened on a Saturday morning, when I'd slept in even later than usual. The girls were sat in front of the TV when I went down, with their empty cereal bowls still on the carpet next to them, and when I looked out of the sitting room window he was there at the top of the garden, hacking away at the trunk of the old hawthorn tree. He'd been worrying away at it for days, cutting back all the branches and burning them on a damp smoky bonfire too close to the house, and slicing his hands to bits on the thorns and dripping blood all over the ground because he couldn't be bothered to wear the perfectly good set of gloves he'd bought from the garden centre. I thought about shouting out of the back door to see if he wanted a cup of tea, but in the end I didn't bother, just made a herbal one for myself in one of the big cups and took it back up to the bathroom for a wallow.

The bathroom's my favourite room in the house. It's tiny, and built in under the eaves, but the previous owners managed to fit in a proper cast-iron bathtub with lion legs – I think it's actually Victorian – that you can stretch right out in, and we treated ourselves to fluffy new towels the girls aren't allowed to use as a moving in present, so my Saturday morning bath is a proper treat. There's no window, just a skylight, so you can lie in there looking straight up at the sky and the clouds passing across above you and keep topping yourself up with hot water and just let everything ebb away.

I'd been there half an hour or more – I remember I was reading one of the colour supplements, not that day's because we hadn't been to the shop yet, but I never get a chance to read the papers on the right day anyway – when I heard Tom talking to someone in the back garden. I couldn't hear what he was saying, and I thought one of the girls must be out there with him, but a couple of minutes later I heard the sound of the back door opening – and felt it too, because it sent a gust of cold air whooshing up the stairs and made me duck down to get as much of myself under the warm water as I could. I heard him telling the girls that he had to go out and to be good and for Maisie to look after her little sister and both of them to look after Mum. And then he was gone.

'Tom!' I yelled down the stairs, but he'd shut the door behind him. 'Tom?'

He wasn't coming back. He had his coat and boots on already, so he had no need to. I sat up in the bath, sending water tsunami-ing up over the edges and onto the cork tiles we were planning to change when we got round to it.

'Tom?' I was bellowing now.

'He's gone out,' called an uninterested Maisie up the stairs.

'Gone out where?' I shouted back down. No answer. The village was a ten-minute drive, and the nearest neighbours weren't much closer, not that we knew them anyway. There was nothing out the back except for the hill.

I stood up in the bath and wrapped a towel round me, managing to dip the corner in the water which made me swear even more. To see anything lower than the very peak of the hill I had to open the skylight, which involved getting out of the bath and slopping even more water all over the place. I could feel myself goosepimpling even before I got the window open and let the November air in to meet my wet hair.

I couldn't see Tom anywhere. There was his axe, lying on the ground next to the jagged stump of the hawthorn tree up by the back wall. He'd finally managed to get it down, and I could see from here the twin circles of its pale flesh shining out brightly from the mossy bark that had enclosed it for so long. He'd made a good start on digging away all the earth around the roots too: I could see their dark writhing shapes exposed unforgivingly to the winter sunlight. There were the black ridges where he had planted his onions and kale and lamb's lettuce, with precious little to show for them save for the labels marking the ends of the rows, and the rainbow spinning windmill Beth had insisted on buying from the garden centre even though there was nothing to scare the birds away from yet. But there was no sign of my husband. I looked all the way up the hillside beyond, still striped and contoured with frost. The sheep had all been taken in for the winter. And for all the woman at the shop said about the views, we'd never seen anyone walking there.

I leaned out of the skylight as far as I dared to look along the ridge to the east and the west. There was nothing but grass and stones all the way to the arching horizon, and nothing but cold grey sky above. The winter sun had barely crested the brow of the hill, and for a moment when I squinted up into its brightness I thought I saw the silhouettes of figures up there, but when I blinked they were gone.

When I got downstairs, still damp, the girls hadn't moved from in front of the television and showed no interest at all in the whereabouts of their father. I pulled on wellies under my dressing gown and walked all the way to the top of the garden shouting Tom's name – thinking all the time how embarrassed I would be if he popped up from somewhere and introduced whatever stranger he'd been talking to with me in that state – but there was no reply except for the wind. When I went back into the cottage I had to switch the TV off to get the girls to even look at me. 'Who was in the garden with Daddy?' I asked them both, but Beth just shook her head dumbly and Maisie, when pushed, insisted she thought he'd been talking to me. I don't think they'd so much as turned away from the screen all morning.

So we waited. Or at least I waited, and tried not to let the girls think that anything was wrong, and when it got as late as I could possibly let it get and still make it to the supermarket – which he knew perfectly well was what we were supposed to be doing that day – I packed them both into the car and drove there and forced myself to go up and down each aisle ticking off every single thing on the list while convincing myself he would be waiting, full of apologies, when we got home. But we arrived back to an empty house, dark and cold, with my note still sitting in the middle of the kitchen table. And that's when I decided to call the police.

Well, you know the next bit. I tried as hard as I could to keep things normal for the girls, but obviously there was nothing normal about their dad not being there and there was nothing I could do to deny it. Every night when I put her to bed Beth asked if her daddy would be back in the morning. Maisie stopped talking about him completely. I think she thought it would upset me. I tried to tell her it wouldn't, but we both knew she was right. Often I'd find her kneeling, staring out of the low back window of their bedroom, a couple of times at night even, long after I thought they were both asleep and there was nothing but pitch blackness on the other side of the glass.

What did I feel? Mostly angry. I was embarrassed about having to rely on people I hardly knew to help me pick up the kids from school and look after them until I could get home in the evening, brilliant as their friends' parents were about rallying round. I was angry about the fact that I had to pack them both into the car and take them with me on a twenty-mile round trip if we needed anything from the shop, or an even longer one if one of them had a play date or a music lesson, and make sure we had enough snacks and books and games to placate the other one who had to sit waiting in the car with me for an hour. I was angry about being left to cope with it all on my own. I didn't sign up for this, I kept saying to myself. I'd put some serious consideration into life as a single parent just a few months before – I'd made lists of the pros and cons and left them out where I knew he would see them so he would realise just how serious a situation we were in – but that had been in London with my oldest friends and my whole support network around me. Not out here in the arse end of nowhere, where you had to spend half an hour scraping ice off the car before you could even get anywhere.

The police didn't start taking it seriously until a fortnight had passed and his bank card and mobile hadn't been used (I'd told them he'd left his phone sitting on the kitchen dresser and even showed it to them, but they said there were still procedures they had to follow). I'd been complaining to Beth's teacher how they hadn't been doing anything at all to look for him and then the very next day on the way to school we drove past a line of police picking their way through the copse near the junction with the main road and a man in a frogman suit stepping down into the dark pond beneath the trees, and it suddenly hit me that this was really happening. I managed to keep things together until I'd dropped the girls off, but I'd hardly got the car out of sight of the school gates before

I had to pull over and spend five minutes dry-heaving into the hedge.

I was saved by the nice lady from the village, the same one who'd told me about the history of the hill. She stopped alongside, took one look at me and put me straight in her 4x4 and drove me back to her kitchen where she made me a strong coffee and insisted I have a tot of something in it, and then she sat down on the other side of the big oak table and ordered me to tell her all about it. Well, it all ended up coming out, about the affair and why we'd moved here and how worried I was about what it was doing to the kids and how terrified I was about what had happened to Tom – all to this woman I barely knew, in fact I'd only found out her name, Vivienne, that very morning – and she just kept handing me tissues and patting my arm, and her dog kept licking my other hand like she was trying to comfort me too, with Vivienne apologising and saying, 'She's too familiar,' and me reassuring her that it didn't matter at all, it was sweet, and by the end of it I felt better than I had in weeks.

It was funny because she couldn't have been less like my mum – Vivienne's country through and through, all gilets and Barbour jackets and sensible boots, and her kitchen was the sort Mum used to be really snobby about, with quarry tiles and an Aga and all these bunches of different herbs, some of which I didn't even recognise, drying above it, and open shelves full of things she had pickled, but right at that moment it felt like just where I needed to be and I've never felt more cared for.

When I'd let it all out she just sat there watching me stroke the dog, and she looked like she was coming to a decision, and then she told me to follow her through to her utility room, which was rigged out with a whelping box full of twelve boisterous springer spaniel puppies that started yapping deafeningly as soon as we opened the door and jumping up at us for attention. Vivienne picked out one – a gorgeous boy with a patch over one eye and a tail going ten to the dozen – and handed him over to me. She told me that she'd heard in the village how my girls had been pushing us for a dog and she thought he might be exactly what we needed right now. And she wouldn't take any money for him, although she did say I could pay her for the sack of food and the bowls and blanket she gave me as well and she'd pass it on to the RSPCA. And as she helped me load it all into the car she said something about 'getting you out with my ladies on one of our nights soon', which was both lovely and slightly frightening – like I say, she was closer to my mum's age than mine – but delivered vaguely enough for the kindness of the offer to take the edge off the actual prospect of it. 'We look after each other here,' she told me as she waved me off. 'You're a part of the community now.'

Well, that sort of restored my faith in humanity and gave me something to go on for. You can imagine how delighted the girls were when they got home and were introduced to the dog, and I told them that yes, we really were going to keep him. And from that day on life felt a bit more manageable and less like we were living on hold, waiting for Tom to walk back in through the door. And Kipper – Maisie let Beth name him, which was really good of her – kept us busy, and cheerful for each other, even when the police liaison officer came to tell me they had drawn a blank on their search of the local area and would be switching over to 'secondary investigation techniques', which as far as I could tell just involved waiting to see if Tom turned up.

Maisie's friend Sarah's parents – it's ridiculous me calling them that, Angela and Julian – were brilliant too, having the girls for the day when I had to go into town and look through the unidentified persons records with the liaison officer to see if Tom was in there, because they knew how upsetting I would find it. They got back at four o'clock absolutely delighted because Angela had taken the three of them out pony-trekking along the ridge. 'We saw our house and we saw you in the garden, and we waved but you didn't see us!' Beth told me, which was confusing, because I'd been at the police station all morning, but Angela just shook her head and told her they had been a

very long way away. Apparently they had planned to go
right to the top of the hill and take a photo of themselves
with the cottage in the background, but Fidget, Sarah's
pony, had gone all skittish so they'd had to turn back
before they'd got there. It seemed like the girls had had
quite enough excitement for one day anyway. They both
went up to bed straight after tea and were out like lights,
although Maisie murmured something weird as I was kissing her goodnight, asking who the other people she saw
in the garden were and saying she had wished for one of
them to be Daddy even though they didn't look like him.

I was determined to make Christmas as normal as
possible for them. The one thing Vivienne had insisted
on was that Kipper shouldn't be a Christmas present – a
dog is for life, etc. – so I'd got them both a Wii between
them as their big present and plenty of other stuff for their
stockings and we'd bought Daddy a *Top Gear* book – it
was Maisie's idea – and wrapped it up and we had a nice
moment putting it on the mantelpiece for him 'ready for
when he comes back'. After breakfast I let them plug in
their new toy and I got on with the dinner. I even checked
Tom's veg patch to see if there was anything I could salvage
for us to have with the turkey, but it was all looking pretty
barren. I'd probably failed to do all sorts of things I was
supposed to over the past few weeks, like watering and
fertilising, what with everything. I think it was the first

time any of us had been up that end of the garden since he disappeared, to tell the truth. Even Kipper tended to skulk round the back of the house to do his wees and poos, helpfully where we were most likely to tread in them. I think he doesn't like the cold, the big wuss. The few times I put him on the lead and took him towards the back of the garden to try to train him to use the big patch of clear earth where the hawthorn's trunk was still lying, he started whining and half throttling himself trying to pull off his collar so he could run back into the house. And I know this makes me a terrible dog owner, but it was too cold to persist for long.

The first Wii argument kicked in after about an hour, and by that time the dinner was at a point where it could look after itself, so I announced that we were all going out for a walk. There was the usual shrieking and wailing, but I silenced that with a reminder of the promises they had made when we got Kipper, and we eventually managed to get ourselves togged out in coats, scarves, hats, mittens and wellies without too much fuss.

To be honest, I didn't blame them when we got out into the weather. It was very much a grey Christmas rather than a white one, with the mist hanging heavy in the valley, but I was fired up by now and I said that rather than take the dog along the lane as usual we were going to walk up the hill. I had an idea that we might be able to get above the fog and see those beautiful views that Vivienne had talked about. She had said she was often up there with her gang, as she called them. But as we trudged up the footpath with the girls discussing their new favourite Mario characters and Kipper doing his best to both strangle himself and trip me up with the lead the fog only got thicker. The footpath was slippy with mud. Beth had a couple of near misses that left her grizzling and complaining, and Kipper nearly had me flat on my face a couple of times, so after a bit I decided we should just strike out across the grass – so long as we were going upwards, we knew we were going in the right direction, after all. The hedgerow soon faded away behind us, and then it was just us trudging across grass stiff and crackly with frost, just the four of us, three girls and a dog, on our own in a world of wet greyness. The girls had stopped talking to save their breath for climbing, and even Kipper seemed to quieten down and settle close to my side in a way that made me think maybe we were getting somewhere with his training after all. He had his ears pressed back hard against his head and he kept darting these quick glances around him. Maybe it was rabbits he could sense out there in the fog.

The hill was higher than it looked. I kept thinking we must be getting close to the top, but then we would suddenly reach an even steeper bit, and I realised we must have got to the fort that Vivienne had talked about.

I wished I'd thought to bring a flask out with us, because the air was so cold up here it felt sharp in the back of your throat, and I was surprised the girls weren't moaning more, but they seemed to have been struck by the same mood as the dog, just huddling into their coats and peering around at the blankness. There was a strange feeling, as if everything – not just us, but the fog and the hill and all the countryside around us – was waiting.

Finally we reached a point where the ground flattened out, and I announced that we had reached the top, although I could see the faint shape of an even higher bit of ground jutting up ahead of us. I had thought to put a couple of mince pies into the pocket of my fleece as a reward, and I was just taking them out and trying with my gloves still on to disentangle the tinfoil I'd wrapped them in when Kipper took fright at something. I saw the hackles bristle all along his little back, and he let out a low growling noise I'd never heard him make before – and then somehow he'd managed to slip the loop of the lead off my wrist and streak off into the whiteness before I could do anything.

Maisie gave a scream. I was shouting his name too, but the racket we were making seemed somehow to dissipate into the mist around us. Beth slipped a small mittened hand into mine, and when I saw her frightened eyes looking up at me, I tried to give it a reassuring squeeze, but my heart was thumping away in my chest and the bloody dog was nowhere to be seen.

I told them both to hush so we could all listen for where he was, and then we could hear him rushing about somewhere, letting out these funny excited yaps and whimpers. But the strange thing was that none of us could agree on where the noises were coming from. I thought he was somewhere on the far side of the hill; Maisie swore blind he had doubled round behind us, and when I asked Beth, all she did was stretch out a shaking arm to point ahead at the place where, now my eyes were getting used to it, there was definitely a higher outcrop rising up out of the mist. It seemed better to be moving in some direction than none at all, so I took both their hands firmly in mine and we started to walk that way.

And that's when we saw Vivienne. This time it was my turn to let out a little scream, because she was standing so still in the gloom I'd thought she was one of the standing stones I was expecting to find up there, and it wasn't until the three of us were practically on top of her that she suddenly stepped forward and said something festive like 'Many happy returns!'

I was so flustered I couldn't think straight, and I blurted out something like 'You're here!'

'We're all here,' she said with that same cheery smile, and I suddenly wondered if it was her dogs that had been making the noises all around us, although I still couldn't see any of them.

'The puppy ran off,' I confessed, feeling like the biggest failure in the world. 'I've lost him.'

'That's boys for you,' she said, in that same strange, detached way that made me think she might have started early on the Christmas sherry. 'They always stray.'

The girls had both gone uncharacteristically shy and were pushing themselves into the back of my coat like they used to when they were tiny. Vivienne squatted down so she was on the same level as them. 'You'll learn that in time, both of you,' she told them solemnly.

'Do you think you can get him to come back?' I asked, trying to ignore how weirdly she was acting. She was, at least, a dog person.

She looked up at me, gave a lopsided smile as if I'd said something funny, and then, with difficulty, straightened up. 'Of course,' she said. 'If that's what you want.' And with that she stuck two fingers in her mouth to let out a whistle so piercing it made all three of us flinch.

Seconds later, up trotted Kipper out of the mist, his ears back and his tail tucked between his legs.

'Thank you,' I gasped as the girls fell on the dog and buried their faces in his damp fur, making affectionate noises that were little more than whimpers. 'How do you *do* that?'

'Magic,' she said, and I started laughing until I realised she wasn't.

The silence grew as thick as the fog surrounding us.

'Now,' said Vivienne finally, clapping her gloved hands together. 'What about Daddy?'

'What d'you mean?' I asked tremulously. But instead of replying to me, Vivienne turned to the girls, who had got a firm hold of Kipper's lead and were standing waiting patiently on either side of him. 'Would you like to see your daddy?'

I wanted to protest, to point out that what she was saying was downright cruel, but the cold seemed to have stolen my voice. So instead I just watched as Maisie, and then Beth, silently nodded.

'Good. Come on then.' Vivienne held out two hands, clad in leather gloves, and the girls slowly reached out to take them and let themselves be led away.

'Where are you taking them?' I croaked as I stumbled along after them, trying to keep them in sight. The close-cropped, wiry grass was icy and slippery underfoot.

'We're going where Daddy was taken,' Vivienne's voice came back through the fog.

'Don't be ridiculous!' I protested, hating the weak voice that was all I could summon up. 'We can't!'

The old woman stopped and turned to face me, her smile radiant. 'Oh, but we can,' she told me, as the girls looked trustingly up at her. 'The old ways are open. Your husband saw to that. And finally we can put the world to rights again.'

'What are you talking about?' I whimpered. But even as I said it, I knew. I was thinking back to those pale twin circles, infinitely ringed, rent apart and broken after so many years. The tree that had stood guardian over our cottage, and over our lives. The only one for miles around.

We were at the very top of the bare hill. And the fog was finally beginning to clear enough for me to make out that what I had thought was just a last outcrop of rock was actually a long barrow, an ancient tomb, just as I had been told I would find up here. And at its nearest end a stone doorway stood open, and there among the pale figures crowded inside—

And then the girls were gone, Maisie hurtling away from us and her little sister stumbling after her as fast as her short legs would carry her, out of Vivienne's grasp and out of my reach and into the white that closed around both of them, crying, '*Daddy, my Daddy!*'

MULTIPLE
OCCUPATION

PEOPLE are always asking how we met, but I've never
actually told the whole story before.

I'd moved up to London the autumn after university
when I got my first job at the agency, and I was living
in a flat in East Finchley. I say flat. It was a bedsit, but
that makes it sound really small and grotty, and it was
actually quite big – I think it must have been the original sitting room of the house, which was one of a whole
street of Victorian or maybe Edwardian houses, proper
old, anyway. It had a big bay window with room in it for
a table and chairs, so it wasn't what you think of when
people say bedsit. The advert in Loot called it a 'Studio
Apartment', but that makes it sound like it was all New
York and *Friends* and bare bricks, which it definitely
wasn't. I was really chuffed with it, though. It had its own
toilet and shower in what was basically a big cupboard,

and proper kitchen units and a worktop against the back wall, even if you did have to clean your teeth at the kitchen sink and spit round the washing up when you hadn't bothered to do it.

It was cheaper than you'd think, because apparently people are funny about living on the ground floor, but it didn't bother me (I always took my laptop into work with me and my stereo was ancient and Dad had managed to put all my stuff on their insurance in any case). Dad took my bed from home apart and brought it down in the back of his car along with some other bits and pieces they said I was welcome to, and then once we'd finally managed to put it back together, he and Mum took me to IKEA to get all the other things I needed. They bought me an Escher print in a frame as a moving-in present, and my friend Sian got me some coloured fairy lights from Woolworths (remember Woolworths?) and we strung them across the bay window and the place started to look properly cheerful.

The hallway was a bit grim – the carpet was all scuffed and there were piles of post sitting out there for tenants who were long since gone. There were four or five different names on the ones addressed to my flat alone. I don't know why no one had thrown them away; most of it was probably junk mail anyway. They made the hallway look really messy and kind of sad. Although the horrible light

out there didn't help either. It had no shade on, and someone had put in an eco bulb – d'you remember the early
ones that were a bit rubbish? – which didn't ever have time
to warm up and start working properly before the timer
switched it off again. I said to Sian that I was thinking
about chucking all the old letters in a bin bag but she said
she thought it might be against the law to interfere with
the Queen's mail. And then she said I should look through
them and see if there were any credit cards or anything
valuable in them I could keep for myself, and I told her
that would *definitely* be illegal, the daffy moo.

The one bad thing about the flat was the noise. Not
from the street – that was quiet, because it didn't really
go anywhere, just looped round from the end of the High
Road and joined onto another road with nothing but
houses on it and the only traffic that really came down
there was people looking for parking spaces. But because
it was just a house that had been divided up, the floors and
the walls weren't exactly designed for keeping the noise
out. I was lucky because the person upstairs didn't play
loud music or anything, but quite often I would wake up
in the middle of the night and hear them talking. To be
fair, it did sound like they were trying to keep the noise
down – they never raised their voice, it was more like a
long, dull monotone – but it started at around midnight
every night and went on and on for what felt like hours at

a time. I figured they must be foreign and making phone calls home then because of the time difference, because there was only ever the one voice, and it definitely wasn't speaking English. Or I suppose they might have been saying prayers.

I'd never actually seen the person who lived there – I figured they must work funny hours, because I'd never bumped into them going in or out. In fact, even though there must have been loads of us living in the building, which was three floors high and had six separate bells next to the front door, the only one of my neighbours I had met was the guy in the room opposite, and we hadn't got any further than saying hello as we passed in the hallway. He had a floppy fringe and a really cute smile, and one time I saw him he was wearing the same top that I was going to get from Urban Outfitters only they'd sold out in my size. And I was pretty sure I'd heard the Pet Shop Boys through his door one night – I wasn't listening or anything, you can't help it when you're in the hallway – which I know doesn't actually prove anything, but still.

Sian got really excited and said I should have a house-warming party and invite everyone in the building so as to get to meet him properly, but I thought knowing my luck he'd be the only one that didn't come, or he'd bring along his girlfriend, or turn out to be a born-again Christian who wanted to tell me the Good News About The Lord or something. And I couldn't exactly picture myself hosting a proper grown-up party anyway. It's easy when you're at university, but I had no idea how ancient some of my neighbours might be.

Besides, everyone says no one in London knows their neighbours. It's like a point of pride, same as banging on about not crossing the river. Sian made a really big deal about how difficult it was to get to north London and visit me even though she'd only been in Peckham for about six weeks.

But I did keep trying to leave the flat at the same time as him in the morning, just so we could say hello in the hallway. And – this is really tragic – I'd got into the habit of not switching the light on in the hallway when I came in at night, so I could see if there was light showing under his door. How sad is that?

So that's what I did after the work party to celebrate us bagging the Longmans account. It was pretty late when I got back – the Tube had stopped running, and I'd shared a taxi with Becky from accounts, who said she could put it on expenses, but I made sure to get in the front because she can be a bit touchy-feely and but-how-do-you-know-if-you've-never-tried when she's drunk. I tried to be really quiet opening and closing the front door so as not to disturb anyone, and, like I say, I'd left the light off (and no, there were no signs of life from his room). I hadn't even got as far as my door – I remember I had my keys out and I was sorting through to find the right one – when I heard someone crying.

I must have jumped at least a foot. You could tell by the sound it wasn't coming from any of the rooms – it was someone actually on the staircase, or one of the landings above. In fact, it sounded so close by I thought there might be someone sitting right at the bottom of the stairs. Except surely then I would have seen them when I opened the front door, because of the light from the street lamps coming in. There was a glass panel in the front door, but once it was shut it only cast a rectangle of orange about as far as the end of the big doormat, and everything beyond that was in total darkness.

I'd stopped dead in the middle of the hallway, halfway between the light switch and my own front door. Should I go backwards or forwards? If I got my door open and the light in my room on, I'd at least be able to make sure there wasn't anyone down there with me. You can see about ten steps before the staircase turns, and I knew logically whoever it was must be further up and the sound of them sobbing was just echoing down from upstairs, but the other thing I kept thinking was that the stairs start literally just beyond the entrance to my flat, and if someone *was* sitting on one of the bottom steps they would be able to reach out and grab my leg while I was trying to get the door open.

So even though I knew it was silly, I went backwards instead. I mean literally backwards, stepping back and reaching behind me to feel my way along the wall. Only I must not have been quite where I thought I was, because when I stretched my arm out I was just grabbing at air, and then I panicked and turned round and ran the few steps to the front door and punched at the big round light switch and of course when it came on there was no one in the hallway and no one on the stairs and everything just looked normal.

And I couldn't hear the crying any more, either. Only I thought I'd heard a sort of gasp when the light came on, and now it had been replaced by that special kind of silence you get when someone is trying really hard not to be heard. Which, come to think of it, was exactly what I was doing.

I knew I ought to say something. Call up the stairs, see if whoever it was was alright. Only it was getting on for one in the morning, on a work night, and I didn't want to piss off any of my neighbours by waking them up. Plus I figured that whoever it was was probably embarrassed at being heard, and the last thing they would want was for me to go thumping upstairs to ask them if they were OK when obviously they weren't, so the best thing was probably for us both to be terribly British about it and for them to pretend they weren't crying and for me to pretend

I hadn't heard them and just get inside my room and get the door locked as soon as possible.

Which is exactly what I did. And I put the chain on as well. And I lay in bed for quite a long time listening and trying to stop shaking, and although I heard what sounded like someone creeping down the stairs at one point and what might have been an outstretched hand scraping along the other side of the wall so as to be sure of their way in the darkness, I definitely didn't hear the front door opening or closing.

I had a stinking hangover the next morning, and when I got back it was already night-time and all I wanted to do was crash out and watch *Wife Swap*, and the next night was Friday and I went out with friends from uni and stayed on Sian's sofa, so it was only when I got back at Saturday lunchtime and found the hallway full of low winter sunlight that I decided to have a look upstairs. I'm not quite sure why, because obviously whoever it was would be long gone, but it seemed ridiculous that I'd been living in the building for months now but I'd never actually been upstairs. There had never been any reason to. So before I could let myself change my mind, I scampered up the first flight to the half-landing. The floor above was a lot darker. There were no windows on this level, because it looked like the landlord had built partition walls out across part of the original landing – you could tell because the fancy plasterwork around the top of the wall stopped, and then started again on the next flight of stairs – and there were just a couple of doors with C and D painted on them. That made sense because I was in B and the fit guy opposite, who I noticed by the way had put up fairy lights in his own window, was A. They were just plain white doors, exactly the same as the ones downstairs, only C – not the one above mine, the other one – had a big crucifix hanging on it, which made me very glad I hadn't gone through with Sian's stupid idea of inviting everyone to a party.

I carried on past them both and up to where the stairs turned again, and I could see another even smaller landing with, you've guessed it, E and F coming off it, only on this level F was at right angles to E, with its walls built out right across almost the whole of the original landing so as to give whoever lived there as much space as possible. But I didn't go any further because I figured if anyone opened their door I couldn't really pretend I was on my way anywhere if I was already on the top floor and it would be really embarrassing, so I came back down again. I did stop for a few seconds outside room D, the one above mine, to see if I could hear anything, but everything was quiet inside.

I was just coming downstairs again when the front door opened and he came in carrying Sainsbury's bags and wearing a really nice blue coat I hadn't seen before and a hat with earflaps on it. He looked slightly surprised to see me, and I blushed bright red, which was ridiculous, and felt I had to explain what I'd been doing.

'I was just having a look upstairs,' I blurted. 'I realised I'd never seen what was up there.'

He put his bags down and stood there and smiled at me, taking his gloves off.

'And it turns out – more stairs!' I grinned inanely. God I was stupid. Why had I even said anything? I didn't need to say anything. 'Only I heard something weird the other night and I—'

'Yeah – what was all that about?' he interrupted me. 'I thought they were going to come through the ceiling at one point.'

'When?' I asked, gormlessly.

'About three o'clockish?'

'Oh – you mean last night? I wasn't here last night, I was staying at my friend's.' As soon as I said it I wondered if he would think I meant the wrong sort of friend, and wanted to kick myself. 'No, I meant Wednesday night. Why, what happened last night?'

He shook his head. 'God knows. Hammering and crashing and all sorts. It sounded like they were doing DIY or something. I nearly went up to tell them to keep it down, only … I don't actually know who lives up there, do you?'

'No, I've never seen them.' He probably thought I was a complete weirdo. Better convince him I wasn't. I'd got to the bottom of the stairs by now and I held out my hand. 'I'm Callum, by the way.'

He had to transfer his gloves to the other hand to shake mine. It was lovely and warm. 'I know, I've, er, seen it on your letters. Robbie.'

'Nice to meet you. I like the lights in your window, by the way.'

'Oh!' Now he was blushing. 'Well, your ones looked pretty cool, so I thought …'

Later on, when I went out to get a takeaway before *X Factor*, I stood in the street and looked at the two sets of illuminations twinkling on either side of the front door. They were the only lights showing in the building.

He looked at my letters, I thought.

X Factor was rubbish, and Sharon Osbourne was on particularly annoying form. I was sitting in the window seat with the curtains not properly closed, partly because I wanted to eat my dinner at the table without getting it everywhere, but also because I wanted to be able to see anyone coming in or out. I was pretty intrigued about the people upstairs now and I wanted to at least know what they looked like. Plus – and even I'll admit this is pretty tragic – I wanted to know if Robbie was going out or not. But it looked like he wasn't. I'd heard the Ant and Dec theme music coming through his door when I got back with my Chinese, so I knew he was at least as cheesy as I was. Which was good, obviously.

I went to bed not long after eleven – I was still feeling the effects of sleeping on Sian's couch the night before – and apart from some drunks shouting out in the street at kicking-out time, everything was quiet.

At least it was until something woke me up a few hours later. I lay there trying to work out what it was. There were muffled footsteps in the room upstairs, like someone was pacing around. But there was a weird scraping noise as well, as if they were dragging something across the floor with them.

The room had got freezing, although I could see from the red light on the electric heater that it was still on. Eventually I was shivering so much that I got out of bed so I could put my hoodie on over my T-shirt and pyjama bottoms, but I couldn't find it until I remembered I'd taken it off along with my coat when I came in and it was still hanging on the back of the door.

I'd just worked it off the peg and was scrambling into it when I heard the crying again. It was muffled by the door but it definitely sounded the same as before. Someone upstairs was sobbing their heart out.

I didn't know what to do. What if it was someone being abused, beaten up by their partner or something? On the other hand, what if it was some nutter who would go off on one, or attack anyone that disturbed them? Should I really get involved? If I did, whoever it was would know exactly where I lived. And if it was just someone who'd locked themselves out of their flat, it wasn't like there was much I could do. The letting agents kept spare keys, but they wouldn't be open until Monday morning now. I really didn't want to have to invite a complete stranger to stay the night in mine. Could I just go back to sleep and ignore it?

At that point, the noise from above started up again. I'd never heard anything like it before. It sounded just like something being hauled across the floor, round and round. Not like someone shifting furniture. More like – and this was a really weird thing to come into my head – an animal pacing around in its cage at the zoo. With its heavy tail dragging behind it. I went across the room to get my phone. It was 2.58.

And at exactly that moment I heard something else: the sound of Robbie's door opening and him calling out, 'Hello?' in a shaky, nervous voice. Which decided it. I went over to the door, unlocked it and peered out.

He only had his door open a crack too, although it was enough to see that he was only wearing a T-shirt and boxer shorts, the clingy trunk kind, not the loose ones. He stared across at me, his eyes wide. I tried to keep mine at face level.

'What do you think's going on?' he whispered. There wasn't really any reason for him to be keeping quiet, given the noise that was now coming from upstairs. The sobbing had got louder – they'd started moaning too, like they were in pain – and as well as the scraping noise from the room above mine I could hear a loud banging, like someone throwing themselves against a door, trying to get out.

'I don't know.' I was shaking even more than before I'd put my hoodie on. I felt the need to be brave for both our sakes, and before I'd really thought about it, yelled, 'HEY!' in the direction of the staircase.

The crying stopped. But the banging didn't. If anything, it got louder.

'It's been going on for ages,' he said. 'Look, the ceiling light in my room's actually shaking.' He opened the door wider and pointed. His room looked nice.

I couldn't think what to do. Are you allowed to phone the police just because someone's making noise?

'I'll come up with you if you want to say something,' I said, kind of hoping he wouldn't. But he just nodded, put his door on the latch and stepped out into the hallway, going over to the front door to switch the hallway light on, for all the difference that made. 'Don't lock yourself out,' he warned me, and by the time I'd sorted out the latch on my own Yale, he'd already started up the stairs ahead of me, which I was quite glad of. And not just for the obvious pervy reason. Believe it or not, the whole situation had freaked me out so much that wasn't even on my mind.

You couldn't see beyond the half-turn in the stairs because of the way the place had been converted, with the walls of Robbie's bedsit built out right up to the banisters, so it was only when I'd made it round the corner and saw him heading straight on up the next flight that I thought I must have made a mistake, because ahead there was nothing but a blank wall where I'd expected to see the doors to the flats on the first floor. I even twisted around to check that I'd already turned and come up two flights, and yes, the hallway was out of sight.

I didn't stop to think for too long, though, because I didn't want to get left behind. Robbie had already crossed the landing and was starting up the next set of stairs, and I had to hurry to keep him in view. The banging noise was even louder up here – it seemed to be coming from behind the wall, which was an obvious modern partition – but then once I'd started climbing again it sounded as if it was coming from the wall to the side of the stairs, and I swear I saw some powdery dust actually shake out of the fancy plasterwork on the ceiling and come snowing down onto the stair carpet. It caught my eye and I was looking down at it which meant I nearly crashed into Robbie's back, because he'd stopped dead on the next landing and was saying, 'That can't be right.'

'What?' I peered round him. There were no doors on this level either. Just another identical turn in the staircase.

'That's what I was thinking,' I started to say, picturing the doors to E and F, and C with its crucifix, which we should already have gone past. And then the lights went out.

Bloody timer switches. It was pitch black. I was holding on to the banister with one hand but without thinking about it I grabbed for Robbie with the other and found the top of his arm and he reached back and held on to my arm too, which was lovely until I realised he was probably just trying to make sure I didn't fall backwards down the stairs. 'Steady,' he said, in a voice that didn't sound it. 'There'll be another light switch somewhere, I'll try to find it. Are you OK?'

'Yeah, I'm fine,' I lied, and felt him let go of me and start groping along the wall ahead. 'Be careful.' I was standing between two steps, a foot on each of them, and clinging on to the banister for dear life.

I could hear him breathing in the darkness, and it took me a second to realise why it was so clear.

'The noises have stopped!' I said, my voice sounding weirdly loud.

'Not all of them,' Robbie muttered from somewhere off to my left. And that's when I realised that the heavy breathing I could hear was coming from somewhere else completely.

'There's got to be a switch on every floor, right?' came Robbie's voice from somewhere even further away. 'I mean, that's just logical, isn't it?'

'Must be,' I said, a lot more confidently than I felt. It didn't feel like logic was a lot of help with what was going on right now.

'D'you want to go back down to the first floor and see if you can find the one down there?' he asked from the darkness.

'No!' I said, slightly too quickly. 'I mean – I think we should stick together.'

'Good idea,' he said, and he sounded relieved.

That gave me the little bit of bravery I needed. I could still hear whoever else it was breathing, and I'd had about enough of it. 'Listen, if there's someone else here, could you do us a favour and hit one of the light switches? We can't find them.'

A faint sob came from below. Which was impossible, because we hadn't passed anyone on the stairs.

'Robbie, come back,' I hissed urgently. And then, more loudly, 'Look, whoever that is, can you stop being a dick and help? This is actually dangerous.'

'What was that?' came Robbie's voice from what sounded like closer by. I stepped up and onto the landing, feeling with my foot to make sure there wasn't another stair to surprise me while groping ahead with both hands to try to find Robbie. We'd both heard what the voice in the darkness said.

'*I tried to put it back. I tried to close it again.*'

'Alright, mate,' I said, not even trying to keep my voice steady now. 'Just switch the lights on. Before someone has an accident.'

'*I tried to close it again,*' the voice repeated, and then it dissolved into that same incoherent sobbing that we'd heard out here on the staircase so many times before.

'Fuck's sake,' I swore, stumbling blindly forward in the blackness. 'Where are you, Robbie?'

'Over here.' He was whispering, but even so his voice sounded further away than I expected. 'I've got to the next lot of stairs. I don't think there's a switch on this floor. I'll go up one more and see if there's one there.'

'Robbie?' I called out, and I could hear the panic in my own voice.

'Yeah?'

'How many floors does this building have?'

'Three, I think.' He had to think about it, and I could tell he was picturing the same view as I was, from the street, with our twin fairy lights twinkling away on the ground floor and the windows on the first floor that never seemed to show any lights at all, and the ones above that on the top floor with the ragged, yellowing curtains permanently drawn across them.

'And which one' – my voice was coming out all high and weird, I didn't sound like me at all – 'which one do you think we are on now?'

I could almost hear him counting in his head. 'But there's another flight of stairs here. I'm standing on the bottom step right now.'

'Come back down,' I said as firmly as I could manage. 'Come back down, we need to go back if we can.' And when I didn't hear him move straight away, I panicked and stumbled forward towards where I thought he must be, only to cry out as my hand made painful contact with something hard.

'Callum? Are you OK? What happened?' I could hear Robbie stumbling towards me in the darkness. My knuckles hurt like hell. I reached out to feel what I had hit, and made out the shape of a door frame, tracing it upwards hand over hand until I found the top above my head.

'Wait,' I found myself saying, and my voice seemed somehow to be coming from a long way away too. 'There is a door after all.'

It still didn't feel right, though. I couldn't work out why, and then I realised: what I was feeling under my hands was not painted wood but cold stone. It had a clammy, damp feel to it.

'There isn't, I worked my way all along that wall,' Robbie said from somewhere behind me, but it didn't seem important now. I was already part way through the doorway. I could feel an icy cold draught washing out over me, and with it there was a smell like damp linen and earth and mould and things that had been locked away for far too long. I took another step forward.

Then suddenly Robbie had grabbed me and wrapped his arms around my chest and pulled me back, and I could feel him breathing sharp and hot against me and that meant we were both alive.

Which is when we heard the stairs above us creaking and the sound of something slowly – stealthily – descending.

We were both gabbling and to this day I've no idea what either of us was saying. Robbie was clutching on to me almost crushingly tight – he says it was to keep me safe; I like to tease him that he was trying to hide behind me – and I grabbed at his arms too and that's when I felt the lump in my hoodie pocket and realised I had put my phone in there when I opened the flat door. Somehow I managed to scramble it out and punch the right buttons to unlock it and bring it blazing into life and throwing out cold white light towards where the ceiling should have been, only it wasn't: there was just a void stretching far above us with a stone staircase that continued to turn and climb endlessly higher and higher, and although we only caught the briefest glimpse of them, there were – it's not the right word, but for want of a better one that may not even exist in our language – *faces* all the way up, leaning out over the rails to look down at us.

But like I say, we only caught a glimpse, because I pointed the light of the phone in the opposite direction, and, both still desperately holding on to each other, we ran for the stairs that led downwards and clattered back down them as fast as we could move. I don't know how we made it without breaking our necks. And I couldn't tell you how many flights of steps there were, or whether there was cold stone or threadbare carpet underfoot at any particular moment, nor how many or how few doors we passed on the way, because I was trying very hard not to look, although I do know the ones there were stood open, and some had figures within them, and some of those figures were reaching out arms and other things towards us.

But we made it to the ground floor, and when we got there it felt the only natural thing to do was to run into the same room together and to lock the door behind us and put the chain on and push a heavy chest of drawers up against it, and stay in there holding on tight to one another all the rest of that night, and then to each pack our stuff and get the hell out of that place the very next morning.

That probably wasn't the sort of story you were expecting, was it? Sorry, hun. But it is kind of romantic, in its own way. Because it's why, to the horror of both sets of parents, we each kissed goodbye to our deposits and clubbed together to rent a two-bedroom, self-contained flat in Highbury that very week. We'd stopped using one of the bedrooms within a month. And after a year we moved into another, nicer place a bit further out along the Victoria Line, and now there's proper scary grown-up talk going on about mortgages and cats and maybe even a wedding at some point.

That means we've been doing quite a bit of looking back at old times recently, so it's fine, don't worry about bringing it all up. Actually, we went back to East Finchley a few weeks ago for the first time in years – we had tickets to see Carly Rae Jepsen at Ally Pally, and yes, thank you, she *slayed* – and we got there early and decided to have a wander and check out some of the places we used to hang out. I didn't really want to go back and look at the old house, but Robbie kept going on about it, and eventually I gave in because I had to admit I was curious too. My only condition was that we didn't knock on the door, and if by some mad chance we were invited, there was still no way I was going inside again.

Well, that didn't turn out to be an issue. Because when we got to the street, the house wasn't there. I mean, literally not there. It hadn't been demolished, there wasn't a gap or anything, and all the other buildings on either side still matched up and looked exactly the same, only they went straight from number 11 to number 15 and there was nothing between them but the alleyway where they kept their bins.

I know!

THE ELF-KIN

IN that land in the far north the nights are dark and they are long, and when winter fastens its jaws about the great forest, it feels it may never let go.

The men of that land are hardy, and they are strong and they are brave, but there is not a soul among them who would let himself be caught beneath the knotted boughs of the trees after darkness has fallen. The mothers call their children in from play the moment that twilight begins to draw out the shadows and thread them together, and there is not a boy or girl who does not heed their first call. Each tries hard not to be the last in the crowd as they hurry back across the snow, and the unlucky soul who finds themselves the hindmost must fix their eyes hard upon the footprints of their playmates, follow as fast as their little legs may carry them, and never, never look behind.

The bolts are drawn across every door in the village before the dusk has even dimmed the snow to grey. All hands in every house rush to light the candles and test the casements before the blackness can thicken and fill the windowpanes. And in each home the fire is stoked till it roars in the hearth. Each father knows he must keep it fed and burning through to dawn, the flames leaping high beneath the chimney's great black mouth. Every mother knows she must keep her candles trimmed and her windows rubbed with whale-oil so nary so much as an icy draught can find a crack to come creeping in. And every child knows that if, in the depths of the night, they should hear a small, cold hand tap-tapping at the glass, they must turn away and wrap their blankets tighter round themselves and stop up their ears. For they must never, never listen to the voices that whisper out on the wind and the whirling snow.

There was a family that lived at the heart of that village. The father was a huntsman, like all the men in those parts, and his son a strapping lad already near six feet tall and fast approaching the age when he too would be blooded in the hunt. The mother had been a beauty in her day, and she kept the remnants of her beauty still, though life in that northern country was not easy, and hers had been harder than some. They had a daughter too, as beautiful as her mother had ever been, and already when she would walk out through the village the boys would laugh and blush to see her, and some of the grown men too.

Her father knew this, and he was proud to see it. And he knew too that the day was coming when a suitor would take her from him, as he had taken her mother from her own father, and as that man in turn had taken his own wife, for this had been the way in those parts for as long as anyone could remember. And earlier that year, when the bite of winter was merely something that hovered between a memory and a suggestion on the north wind, he had strapped on his boots and his travelling coat, loaded up the sled with bearskins and wolfskins and barrels full of smoked meat, and left his family for the long journey to the trading post with a special purchase in his mind. Returning after three long weeks, he brought with him the usual provisions of oil and spice, of liquor and linen, and of musket pellets, tobacco and trinkets that his family fell to cooing over, but he brought back a special package too, one which stayed wrapped in its waxed paper and ribbon and was even now tucked away in the topmost drawer of the linen press where only he knew. A beautiful gown all stitched in gold, the finest he could buy, and a pair of silk slippers with beads of coloured glass that sparkled in the light.

For it was fast approaching the low time of the year, when the villagers would exchange gifts and good wishes for the return of the sun and the summer when it was at its most distant. But the shortest day cannot come without the longest night, and that, in that village at the heart of the great dark forest, was the time of most danger.

For that far north land is riddled with the elf-kin. They hide themselves in the gnarled trunks where the trees press close in the forest, pursuing a hunt of their own. They bury themselves deep in the slippery leaf mould beneath the crust of the snow to pull down unwary travellers to join them. And they seek out the places in ill-kept homes where the wood is rotten and bad, and they push themselves into the cracks and bring sourness and blight in their wake.

But the longest, darkest night of the year is when the lord of all the elves himself rides out, looking for children to snatch from their homes. And though no man, woman or child alive can say they have caught so much as a glimpse of him, they say you will know him by his wild white hair and terrible laugh, and by the cloak he wraps tight around himself. For it is as red as blood.

The family were well prepared for his coming that year. The father set to chopping wood all day, his axe flashing red in the light of the dawn and the sunset too. The son trudged back and forth from axe block to house, his arms filled with logs, so the fire would be well stocked all through the long night. The mother busied herself at the stove, and the daughter helped her to butcher the deer that had hung in the cottage for seven full days now, and mixed the blood for the puddings herself, for her father insisted she learn the skills that would make her a good wife when that day came.

The peaks of the snow still showed rose in the light of the dying sun when the father closed their door and pulled the great bolts across it, and he carried the largest midwinter candles himself and set them in their places on the window ledges as the light beyond faded to blue and on into blackness. Then he bade the mother and the daughter take off their bloody aprons, and the son take off his boots and his cap, and all kneel at the hearth with him at prayer.

'Let this our family circle be joined, and never rent asunder,' he said, 'and should anyone have sins to confess, let them confess them now.' And the candle in the left-hand window sputtered and went out.

'Mother, you have not trimmed your wicks well,' he scolded, getting to his feet and snatching up a taper to relight it. But although there was a good length of wick, and more when he took his knife to the candle-tip to shave it, it would not light again. It would only spark and give off a foul smell.

The father bade them kneel again and bow, forcing his children's heads down with his rough hands. Again he said, in a louder voice this time, 'If any in this family have sins to confess, let them confess them now, lest the elf-kin take them.' And although the mother and the daughter tried to keep to their prayers they could not help but open an eye to look to the candle in the right-hand window, so they both saw it flicker as if caught in a great gust of wind, and go out.

This time the father did not leave the hearth, though he leaned forward to hurl a fresh log into the heart of the fire. He pushed his children's heads down until they were brushing the floorboards, and he said once more, in a voice which echoed throughout the darkened house, 'Confess to your sin.' But his family said nothing, and all that could be heard was the wind.

So the family knelt on in silence, as the flames that had leaped up towards the great black mouth of the chimney only minutes before fell back and sank into the glowing ashes. And the embers themselves began to lose their glow, and a cold blackness closed on the room.

The father's voice was hoarser now. 'Speak!' he ordered. 'For surely one of you has sinned.'

And at that moment a spark seemed to catch in the dying fire, and a glowing ember loosed itself and floated out into the room above their heads. It was not orange, as would issue from an ordinary fire, but a bright white. And it did not dance in the air like an ordinary ember, but bore steadily out across the room, and up to the linen press on the far wall where it lingered at the topmost drawer.

The father let out a roar, and he strode to the press and yanked it open. Inside lay the package, still in its waxed paper and tied with a ribbon, but even with his rough ways he could see that the paper was crumpled and the ribbon retied by a clumsy hand that belonged to no shop-keeper. He caught up the package in one hand and took his daughter by her hair with the other, pulling her to her feet as she let out a scream.

'Confess!' he urged her, brandishing the package in her face. 'You have sought out the gift that should have been thine, and have been looking upon it with covetous eyes! Well, for your pride, you shall not have it!' And though it had cost him dear, he made to throw the gown and the silk slippers, paper and ribbon and all, onto the fire, which let out a little heat still. But his hand was stopped by another scream, and this one came from his wife.

'What is it?' he hissed as he looked at her in the light of the low flames. But the woman had clamped both her hands to her mouth, as if to stop any further noise issuing from it.

The man let go his daughter, who fell back sobbing on the hearth. And he crossed instead to his wife, and hauled her up by the shoulder. 'So, it is you, is it?' he demanded. 'Could you not bear to see your own daughter's beauty? Are you so envious? Did you think you should have it yourself?' And he drew back his arm and gave her such a blow across her face that it swelled and bloodied her eye and she fell sobbing to the floor.

At that the light of the fire dipped yet lower, so that the family could barely see one another. But the father's rage was still blazing. And he spoke to his son without looking at him, saying, 'Fetch my whip, boy.'

But his son's voice came back from the darkness: 'I will not.'

Still the father did not turn, for he was looking down at the sobbing women at his feet. 'What did you say to me, boy?' he said in a voice that was low like the growl of a bear.

'I will not fetch your whip, Father,' said the son in a voice that quavered between the reedy treble of a boy and the boom of a man, but was ever firm. 'For it is I that have sins to confess.'

'Speak them then, boy,' snarled his father, who knew full well that for many long years he had been the only one tall enough to reach the topmost drawer of the linen press.

'It was I who was covetous, Father. For I looked upon the package, and I wished it might be mine.'

There was so little light in the room now that all the boy could see was the shape of his father towering over the women where they lay in front of the fireplace.

'It was I who was envious, Father. For I took out the gown, and I ran my fingers over its golden stitching, and I wondered how it would feel it against my skin.'

The very last light of the embers showed the black mouth of the chimney gaping wide.

'It was I who was proud, Father. For when I took down the silk slippers, with their beads of coloured glass that sparkle in the light, they fitted me perfectly.'

And at that the father turned, and whip or no whip he raised his arm to strike his son with all the force that was in him. But the boy did not flinch, and although the tears ran down his face, he stood firm, and shouted into his father's face in a voice which cracked and fluted:

'I have listened to the voices on the wind, Father. And they are full of music. And there is laughter!'

And at that moment the cottage was plunged into a blackness so total that the father could not tell up from down or which from what, and a great whirling wind and mass of choking ashes filled the air around him, and a terrible roaring laughter seemed to come from everywhere at once. The boy felt a pair of arms, as strong as knotted oak branches, fasten about his waist, and as he was pulled backwards and upwards it was all that he could do to reach out in the darkness and clutch his sister's hand in his left and his mother's hand in his right and hold on to them as tight as never-let-go.

In that land in the far north the nights are dark and they are long, and when winter fastens its jaws about the great forest it feels it may never let go. The men of that land are hardy, and they are strong and they are brave, but there is not a soul among them who would let himself be caught beneath the knotted boughs of the trees after darkness has fallen. For that far north land is riddled with the elf-kin. They hide themselves in the gnarled trunks where the trees press close in the forest, pursuing a hunt of their own. They bury themselves deep in the slippery leaf mould beneath the crust of the snow to tempt unwary travellers. You may hear their music and laughter on the wind and the whirling snow. And although no man alive will admit they have caught so much as a glimpse of them, they say that you will see them sometimes in the distance, in the shadows of the trees or just beyond the candlelight that spills from your window.

They say that their lord wears a cloak as red as blood. And they say that among his retinue there are two ladies, an old one and a young one, whose beauty is beyond telling. But the tallest and most beautiful of his companions is clad in a gown with golden stitching, and when he passes over the snow his silken slippers leave no footprints.

THE LILY-WHITE BOY

HE hadn't been able to use the rear-view all the way up because of Jack's stuff piled in the back, and it wasn't until they were nearly halfway home that he realised how nervous he'd been, having to rely on just his side mirrors.

When they got in she went straight to the kitchen to put the kettle on. When she brought him his tea, he was sitting there with his coat still on.

'He'll be having his dinner now I expect,' she said as she worked her way round the lounge switching on lamps and drawing down the blinds. 'It looked alright, that canteen, I thought. I don't expect he'll ring till tomorrow, he'll be settling in. I thought we could just have something out of the freezer.'

'Whatever's easiest,' he told her, and he reached for the remote control.

*

Jack didn't call until the Thursday, when they were just settling down to their tea. He kept an eye on the pans while Susan talked to him and the sauce was just beginning to stick on the bottom when she called him through to have a word.

'Don't waste your money; your mother'll tell me your news,' he said as soon as he picked up the receiver from the hall table. 'How are you getting on? OK?'

His son sounded echoey and far away. 'It's great, Dad. Really cool. I've met some really nice people, and my room's fine, and I'm going to the try-outs for the football team tomorrow.'

'And how about the work?'

'Well, lectures don't start till next week, but I've met my tutor and she seems really nice.'

'That's good. They'll keep you busy, I expect. Well, I mustn't keep you. Are you out tonight?'

'I thought I might go down the bar.'

'Alright. Well, enjoy yourself. Remember your money's got to last you the whole term.'

'Yes, Dad.'

When he put the phone down she was watching him from the kitchen. 'You didn't have to be so quick,' she said. 'We got him that card, remember?'

'Aye, well.' He took the plate she was holding out for him. 'He's got more important things to do than spend ages gabbing to us. He's off out, anyway.'

'Is he? I hope he's being sensible. Hurry up now, that thing's on you wanted to watch.'

He had done all the Brainteasers by the time she went for a shower on Monday morning, and when she came out he was making a start on the crossword. He didn't even like crosswords.

'What are you going to do today?' she asked him while she looked round for her keys.

'Oh, I don't know.' He folded the paper in half and looked at her over the top of his glasses. 'There's that fence at the back. And I suppose I ought to check the guttering before the winter.'

She checked in her bag for a packet of tissues. 'Why don't you make a start on that stuff from your mum's in the loft? You could move some of the boxes down into Jack's room while you sort through them and decide what you want to keep.'

She saw him bristle, and wished she could bite back her words.

'That's his room for as long as he needs it. I'm not filling it up with our stuff. What if he wants to come home for a weekend?'

'Alright then.' She smiled meekly and went in for a kiss. He gave her his cheek, and shook out the paper with a grunt, trying to think of a (6,4) phrase that meant 'shapely manoeuvres a hit with military'.

He didn't get up to the loft until the following week, when the weather made getting anything done in the garden impossible. He felt even closer to the rain up here with it drumming on the tiles just a few inches above his head, but thankfully it didn't seem to be coming through anywhere. There was no sign of mice, either, which was a relief.

The boxes from his mother's were not far back – they had only cleared out her house in February – but Jack had dumped a load of his stuff in front of them, lazily blocking the duckboards which were the only safe path down the middle of the loft instead of balancing it across the joists under the eaves like everything else. There was his old Dungeons & Dragons stuff (he had been mad about that for a couple of years), some bin liners full of clothes he wouldn't wear any more, CDs he didn't want his friends at university to know about, and a box of books too. He spent a while leafing through *The Jungle Book* in the light of the single 60-watt bulb, smoothing out the dog-eared pages and remembering how they had read it together when Jack was little enough to tuck into the crook of his arm and carry up the wooden stairs to Bedfordshire once his head had started to droop into his chest.

When he had shifted Jack's stuff to where it ought to have been in the first place, there was a gap just wide enough to drag his mother's boxes through to the trap-door. One of them seemed to have split, and it left a trail of reddish dust, or maybe rust, on the boards behind it. He would have to bring up a dustpan and brush later. But when he got it to the edge of the trapdoor and had to hold it awkwardly over his head in order to hoist it down, thankfully there didn't appear to be anything leaking from the bottom. He dumped it on top of a spread-out newspaper once he got it down to the lounge, just in case.

It took him three more trips to get everything down, and when he was gathering the last bits and pieces together he thought he heard a noise from downstairs. He called out 'Hello?', thinking that maybe Susan had popped back for her lunch, and even stuck his head through the trapdoor to peer down at the landing, but there was nobody there. He was hearing things now. He was finding it hard to get used to how quiet the house seemed without Jack in it.

It was only after he had closed the trapdoor and put the ladder away that he realised he had forgotten about the dustpan and brush. Oh well. It would wait.

*

When she got home from work he was poring over the old family Bible, with the photographs in the front going all the way back to Victorian times. 'Look,' he told her. 'I haven't seen these in years. She must have had them when *her* mother died.'

She was dying for a cup of tea, but it was so nice to see him enjoying something that she popped her reading glasses on and sat down next to him. 'Who've we got, then?' she asked, pointing to a girl in a white dress sitting on a high stool. 'Is that your grandmother?'

'No,' he chuckled. 'That's a little boy. My Great-Uncle William. I never knew him, he was killed in the war.'

'Oh, yes, I'd forgotten they used to put the boys in pinafores too. Oh, look at his little face! He doesn't look too pleased to be having his picture taken, does he?'

He smiled. 'None of them do. Look at them. Miserable as sin. I think it's because they had to sit still for so long. Look, here's Nana.'

'Oh, wasn't she pretty.' The girl bore no relation to the sour-faced old woman she remembered from their engagement party, though she had spoken barely a word to her. She had nearly spoiled the wedding, too, dropping dead just a month before with the church all booked and the dresses all ordered, and they had worried they might have to cancel, though Colin himself had not seemed that upset, saying they had never been close.

She hadn't thought about her in years. 'How old is she there?'

He peered at the inscription beneath the photograph. '1916. So she would have been' – he consulted the family tree at the front of the book – 'eighteen. I wonder what the occasion was?'

They peered at the long white dress with its corsage of lilies. 'Could it have been her engagement?' Her own was still at the front of her mind.

'No, she didn't marry Grandpa till years after. It's in here. 1926. And besides, he'd be in it too, wouldn't he?'

She pursed her lips. 'Not necessarily. He might have been away in the war. And she might have had this photo taken for him, so as he could carry it in the pocket of his uniform, to remember her by.'

He smiled at her. 'You've been at the Catherine Cooksons again. D'you want a cup of tea?'

'Go on then.' She took the book from him as he stood up and slid it onto her own lap. 'Could it have been, though?'

'I don't think so. I think she met Grandpa through the church, and Mum said they married and had her quite quickly because by then Nana was already getting on for thirty, and that was late to be having kids in those days.'

'Hmm.' She gave one last disappointed glance at the

picture before turning the page and, as she did so, a piece of stiff card dropped out and slid to the carpet.

'What's this?' she asked him when he came back in with the tray. She had put the photograph on the arm of the sofa. There didn't seem to be an obvious place in the book for it to have fallen out of.

'Oh, I don't know. It was tucked into the same page as the picture of Nana. I suppose they didn't bother to mount it because of the face.' The picture was of a young man in army uniform standing in front of the usual painted backdrop, but although his tunic and puttees and even the badge on his caps could be seen clearly, where his face should have been there was just a blank white space.

'I wonder if somebody scratched it out,' she commented, swapping the picture for the packet of chocolate Hobnobs he was holding out to her.

'I don't know.' He ran his thumb across the surface of the photograph. 'It doesn't feel like it. It looks more like light shining off him. Did they have flash in those days? I suppose they must have had, mustn't they? Or perhaps something went wrong with the processing. Either way, they can't have been pleased. Look, it's in a studio, they must have paid good money for it.' He turned the card over. The name of the company inscribed on the back meant nothing to him. But there was something else there, in spidery pencil that he had to hold up to the light of the window to decipher. 'It says … Tommy, I think it is. Look, here, very faintly. I don't remember a Tommy. Have a look in the family tree.'

She wiped the last traces of biscuit from her fingers with a tissue before leafing back through the pages of the Bible. 'No. William's here, the brother – killed at Flers, 1916 – but no Tommy. What was your granddad's name?'

'Bert,' he said, so that settled that.

She was looking down at the family tree, tracing the branches with her finger. She found her own name etched at the bottom in biro: *m. Susan Spencer 1976*. 'You should update this,' she told him. 'Put Jack on, and Sarah's lot. You could even take it back further. They have all sorts on the internet these days, you can go back centuries. Carol at work was telling me she's doing theirs.'

'Hmm.' He was still staring at the photo in the last of the day's light coming in through the window on the western front of the house. 'Maybe.' He slipped it absently into the breast pocket of his shirt and rubbed his hands together. 'I think I might put the heating on tonight. It's cold in here, isn't it?'

'You wouldn't believe it if you could see me,' he told Jack. 'They've got all these records available, and I found your great-grandmother on there, and her brother and mother and father.' No Tommy, however – not that that was worth mentioning to Jack. 'He was a stonemason, it turns out, your great-great-grandfather. You have to pay extra to get a printout. I'm going to order some next time I'm online.'

His son chuckled at the end of the line. 'I never thought I'd hear you say "online". The way you used to shout at me to get off the internet and stop wasting money when you wanted to use the phone!'

'Aye, well, this is useful stuff I'm doing, not just *surfing*.' He smiled. 'For stuff further back than that you have to go to the Public Record Office, so we're thinking of getting the train down to London one week when your mum's got a couple of days off and staying with Sarah and her lot.'

'Wow. You're taking it really seriously.'

'It's interesting. Well, I find it interesting.' He felt suddenly bashful, embarrassed by his enthusiasm. 'What have you been up to, anyway?'

'I went on a march on Saturday,' Jack told him. 'Against them bombing Iraq. The student union organised a coach and we all went down to London.'

'Did you?' He was surprised, and a little uneasy. His son had never struck him as particularly political.

'Uh-huh. And I've signed the petition. It's online. I'll have to email you the link now you know how to use it. Did you know they're thinking of bringing back the draft in America?'

'Are they? I've not read about it in the paper.'

Jack sounded exasperated. 'No, well, it's hardly been reported. But it's in front of the Senate, or Congress, or whatever. And if it happens there, it's only a matter of time before it happens over here.'

'Oh, I don't think you need to worry about that.' He suddenly felt sick in the pit of his stomach. 'I can remember the fuss when they got rid of National Service, I'm sure they wouldn't want to bring it back again.'

'You didn't have to do it, did you?' His son sounded curious.

'No, no, they got rid of it long before I was old enough. Your granddad did, though. He was in the Royal Engineers just after the war. I remember him taking us to Aldershot to show us his old barracks. And my uncle Graham was out in Malaya. And it turns out my great-uncle – that would be your great-great-uncle—'

'Enough family tree!' Jack protested, laughing.

'Alright, alright,' he smiled. 'You look after yourself, anyway. D'you want to speak to your mother again before you go?'

Susan stubbed her toe on one of the boxes when she was on her way to bed, and because she was only wearing her bunny slippers, it really hurt. 'Right, I want these shifted,' she told him, leaning on the computer table and trying to pinch some of the pain out of her foot. 'You've had them down here nearly three weeks. Jack's not coming home till the holidays, he's said he's too busy, so you can put them in his room in the meantime. No arguing. Alright?'

'I've not even looked in that one yet,' he said guiltily. 'I'll move them first thing in the morning.'

They went up to bed. There were the usual night-time sounds of running water, and Colin setting the alarm, and the floorboards in the bedroom creaking. One by one, their lamps went out. Soon the only sounds in the place were the clicks and gurgles of the central heating as the system switched over to economy seven, and the only light came from the clock on the video in the lounge and the thin strip of moonlight that slipped between the curtains and stretched across the hearthrug and halfway up the scuffed magnolia on the far wall. As the night wore on, it worked its way slowly across the room, striping each of the cushions on the sofa in turn and inching across the side table with its neatly stacked pile of ceramic coasters until it illuminated the cardboard boxes stacked in the corner, beside the desk where the computer stood.

The machine started up without a sound. Its screen glowed white for a moment, a cold bright rectangle in the darkness, but just as soon as the light had built up to its full intensity it faded away again, leaving a blank frame in the corner of the room.

The digital figures on the video silently rearranged themselves: 05:00.

*

Sergeant says we go over the top at dawn: oh-five-hundred hours as the army insists on calling it but a d—n silly time to be up in anyone's language and an even d—n sillier thing to be doing in it. One of our lads came up the line from Pozières yesterday – poor sod, I think he thought he was out of it for the foreseeable, but they just patched him up and packed him straight back down here with his arm in a sling, saying they'd give him a Webley instead of his rifle because you only need one hand to fire them and they knew he would want to do his duty alongside his comrades. Anyhow, he was talking to some of the lads in the clearing station who'd been up at the front there and they said Jerry looks to be in pretty bad shape – we've had our Jack Johnsons pounding him for three or four nights making a hellish noise that you wouldn't believe, so maybe, just maybe, tomorrow'll be the push that takes us there. That's what the lieutenant keeps telling us, anyway. Myself, I won't believe it until I'm sipping a beer and writing you a postcard from sunny Berlin, but what do I know.

'I thought you were supposed to be moving that stuff, not reading it,' said Susan, brushing her hair as she came into the lounge.

'Hmm? Mm. Going to. It's just – there's a lot of stuff here in the box I haven't been through yet. I think it might be the answer to our little mystery.'

'Oh, the unknown soldier?' She walked over and stood beside him, looking down at the yellowing paper in his hand.

'Yeah. It's a letter. There were a load of them in there, all tied up with ribbons, you'd love it. I think all the stuff in there came straight from Nana's. I'm not sure Mum even opened the box.'

'And who are they from?'

He turned the letter over in his hand. 'Private T.A. Boscombe, 13th Service Battalion of the Cheshire Regiment. Or *"forever your own Tommy"* if you prefer.'

She looked delighted. 'So there was a sweetheart!'

'Looks like it. I guess he didn't make it through the war, though. This is the last of the letters.'

'Oh, how sad. Has it got a date on it?'

'November 1916. Doesn't say where he was, though. I expect they censored that sort of thing.'

'But it would be easy enough to find out, wouldn't it, now that you know what regiment he was in. Look, I must go, the traffic's been murder this week. And I still want this stuff shifted!'

He kissed her goodbye and listened as her heels clicked down the driveway and the car reversed and disappeared off up the street. It sounded a bit off, he thought. Be worth checking the brakes when he had a chance. It was due for a service soon anyway.

He returned to the letter.

This will make you laugh. Or maybe it won't, I don't think I've got a very good idea any more of what's funny or not after ten months out here. I was talking to one of our fellows the other day, a lieutenant who's been interrogating a lot of the prisoners down at GHQ – he speaks good German, was a sales clerk for Lever's before all this began – and guess what their lot call the trenches? Schützengraben, if you can get your tongue round that. And it's because a graben means a grave in German. Think of that! Sometimes when I'm standing to out there in the freezing cold with the water up to my ankles and the rats swarming round my feet and the stink rolling in of all the bodies that are lying out there, the only thing you want to look at is that rectangle of sky above the top of the trench with the clouds still scudding by as if everything was normal down beneath them, and that's where I think I am. Already in the grave, and they're just saving time by sending me there early.

Forgive the ramblings of a lonely soldier. You mustn't worry about me. Will has promised to look out for me, and I have promised to look out for him, and I know in your prayers you are looking out for both of us. He is a good man, your brother, and I will be proud to have him standing beside me when the order comes and we go over the top together. And no doubt the lieutenant is right, and this will be the push that ends it all, and Will and I will be back before you know it. Back from our grave, and home where we belong. And know this: whatever the dawn may bring, I will always be

Forever your own

Tommy.

'I put all that stuff back up in the loft,' he told her that evening, as he fiddled with the thermostat. 'I don't think I'm going to carry on with it, to be honest. What is wrong with this thing? We never had any problem last winter. It can't be on the blink already.'

'Why not?' she asked him, surprised. She was folding towels ready to go in the airing cupboard.

'I don't know. It just seems like it might be better to leave some things as they are. I mean, Nana obviously never wanted us to know about this Tommy, did she? I don't think she ever told Mum about him.'

'Your mum had the letters,' Susan pointed out.

'Yes, but that was in the stuff we cleared out from *her* attic. I don't reckon she ever even looked at them. She never said anything about it. What if she *did* look at them, and it upset her?'

'Why would it upset her? Here, help me with this.' She passed him the end of one of the big bath sheets.

'Well ...' he said, and tailed off, thinking. 'If he hadn't been killed, she would have married him instead of Grandpa, and Mum and Sarah and me and Jack wouldn't even exist!'

'Yes, but he was, wasn't he? And you do. It's just the sort of thing you expect to find out about when you do your family tree. It's fun!'

'Hmm.' He didn't look convinced.

'Well, I think it would be a shame to stop. You were enjoying it so much.' She picked up the pile of laundry and walked up the stairs. 'God, look at this! It's no wonder you can't get the place warm!'

He followed her out. She was looking up at a black rectangle above her head. 'You've forgotten to put the trapdoor back over!'

He stared up into the darkness. 'But I'm sure ... I remember ...'

'Oh, go and fetch the steps. That's where all the heat's going, up there!'

But when he went up the ladder it didn't feel like there was any heat in the attic at all. Quite the opposite, in fact. There was an almost tangible chill rolling out of the black hole above his head. He could see his breath clouding in front of his face as he came level with the frieze that ran round the top of the wallpaper on the landing, and he stopped, clutching the ladder in sudden fright.

What was this? This was ridiculous. He was a grown man, and he'd never been afraid of the dark. But he was no more willing to put his head up into that cold blackness above the rim of the trapdoor than he would have been to let go of the ladder and tip himself over the banister twenty feet down into the hallway below. What the hell was wrong with him? What did he expect to happen? The light switch was only a couple of feet above the trapdoor, attached to one of the roof beams; he had reached up and pressed it a thousand times without even thinking. He knew perfectly well what was waiting for him in the darkness – only the boxes and bags he had been up there shifting around a few hours before.

Forcing himself to smile at his own stupidity, he screwed his eyes shut and groped upwards with a trembling hand for the handle of the trapdoor, holding on tightly to the cold metal of the ladder with his other hand. He was letting out his breath in little sharp gasps, all his senses straining for the tiniest noise, the slightest sensation from the blackness above. And all he could think was *If something reaches out and touches my arm right now* – but then his grasping fingers found the knob on the trapdoor and he pulled it towards him just as a board creaked a few feet away from his head and something started to move across the attic.

'What was that noise? You didn't fall, did you?' asked Susan, appearing at the foot of the stairs.

'No – no, just came down the ladder a bit quick. Thought there was another step,' he gasped, drawing back into the doorway to Jack's room so that she wouldn't see the clammy sweat that had erupted on his forehead, in his armpits and in the small of his back. 'All sorted now. I'll put this ladder away in the garage, I think. We're not going to need it for a while.'

The shopping centre was crowded – Christmas shoppers, she supposed, even though it was barely the second week of November – and the only table was right in the far corner of the food court, and it hadn't even been cleared. It was only after they had shifted the dirty cups to the side and unloaded their own trays and pushed their bags well in under the table where no one could make off with them that she told Carol what was on her mind.

'I'm worried about Colin,' she said as she split the foil top on the tub of milk and spiralled it into her coffee. 'He's having trouble sleeping. The number of times in the last couple of weeks I've woken up in the middle of the night and found him just lying there, wide awake, staring up at the ceiling. I keep telling him to go to the doctors, but he won't listen.'

Her friend smiled. 'Oh, they never do, do they? When Rob's back went, it was a week before he'd admit there was anything wrong, and even then I had to drive him down there or I don't believe he'd have gone in. Is he worrying about something?'

She shook her head, lifting the cup to her lips but finding it still too hot to drink. 'I don't think so. Not that he'll talk about, anyway. I think he misses Jack more than he'll admit. He's been quiet ever since he went off to university.'

Carol nodded. 'They're close, aren't they?'

'Always were. And … I don't know. I think when Jack was coming and going all the time it sort of gave Colin some structure to his day. You know I was worried when he took early retirement that he wasn't going to find enough to do with himself. That's why I wanted him to get going on the family tree stuff.'

'He's not kept up with it?'

'No, he seemed to lose interest. He was so enthusiastic about it to start with. We were even going to have a trip down to London. Then he just sort of … turned in on himself. He sits around all day. He's stopped getting up in the mornings when I go to work, which is fair enough because he's so tired all the time, but the other day I swear he didn't get up at all. He was still up in the bedroom when I got home, and he hadn't even shaved. I'm really worried about him, Carol.'

Her friend gave her a reassuring smile. 'Well, we should be able to sort out the sleeping thing, at least. Valerian's very good for that. We've got time to get across to Holland and Barrett before we're due back.'

She smiled, grateful that at least her friend was taking the problem seriously. 'Thank you.'

'Oh, don't be daft. I've been taking it for months for my hot flushes,' her friend grinned, slipping off her winter coat and stowing it on the back of her seat, tweaking the crumpled red flower that was pinned to the lapel as she did so. 'Oh, just look at the state of this poppy. They always get tatty, don't they? It feels so disrespectful.'

'Oh, I feel terrible, I haven't got one yet.'

'You can get one here, I saw the man earlier. Where's he got to?' She craned round, scanning the crowded mall. 'That's weird. He was over there, dressed up in one of the old-fashioned uniforms. I saw him when we were trying to find a seat. He was staring right over here, I thought he must have his eye on one of the waitresses.'

Susan gazed around at the milling shoppers and shook her head. 'It doesn't matter. There's always someone at the station, I can pop in on the way home. Come on, or we'll never get back to work in time. What did you say this stuff was called?'

She posted an advent calendar off to Jack at university. It was silly, she knew, but she thought it would probably make him laugh, and anyway, he would appreciate the chocolate.

Colin was still lying there on his back when she came back from brushing her teeth, just staring up at the ceiling.

'Did you have another bad night, love?'

He nodded, without even looking at her.

'Oh, I'm sorry.' She sat down on the bed beside him, stroking his bald patch. 'D'you think you managed to drop off at all?'

'Don't think so.' His mumble was almost unintelligible.

She glanced across at the clock on the bedside table. She was going to be late again. 'Look, why don't you come down and meet me for lunch today? We could pop into Boots in the arcade and see if they can recommend anything stronger. I thought those things of Carol's might start working if we gave them a few weeks, but they don't seem much good, do they?'

He shook his head emphatically, rumpling the pillow. 'No. Not today. I can't go out. Not feeling like this.'

She balled her fists, digging her nails into her palm, but when she spoke she managed to keep her voice calm. 'Well, why don't you try to have a bit of a nap this morning, and see how you feel later? I'll give you a call from the office.'

He scowled up at the ceiling. 'No. You get on. I'll stop here. It'll be OK.'

'I …' She really did have to go. She shook her head. 'I'll give you a call later anyway. Maybe go out for a walk or something. The fresh air might help.'

He listened to the sound of her car as she pulled out of the drive.

'And you're sure I'm doing the right thing?'

Carol glanced round the office to check there were no supervisors lurking before scooting her swivel chair over to Susan's side of the desk and taking her friend's hands in her own. 'Look. You need to do this for your own sanity, if not his. There's no shame in it these days. Look at Robbie Williams. He'll thank you for it in the long run, I promise you.'

Susan nodded.

'Now, go on and get it done while her highness isn't around to listen in on you. I'll make us both a cup of coffee while you're doing it.'

She punched in the number from the piece of paper

she had been carrying around in her handbag for a week or more. The receptionist answered on the first ring.

'Hello. Oh hello. It's Susan Baxter here. I wondered if I could make an appointment with Dr Virdi. I … it's actually my husband I need to talk to him about.'

Colin sat on the edge of the bed, his hands on his knees, absolutely still, his face turned up to the ceiling. He had an idea that the thing in the attic only moved when he moved, so he was concentrating every ounce of his will on maintaining his position, ignoring the pins and needles which were creeping maddeningly in his legs and the cramp in his neck, and straining his ears for the slightest sound from above, so when the phone rang and shattered the silence it was like an electric shock running through his body.

'Hello?'

'Dad?'

'Jack?'

'Sorry, were you out in the garden?'

'What?'

'It just took you a while to answer. I thought you might have been gardening.'

'N-no. I was just – sorry. I was doing something.' He glanced out through the patio doors at the garden. It was already getting dark. Susan had been nagging him about getting out there and raking up the leaves that morning. Or it might have been the day before. Too late now, anyway. He pulled the telephone cord to its full length so that he could stand at the bottom of the stairs and keep an eye on the trapdoor while he was talking.

'Oh. Well, I just – how are you? OK?'

'Fine. Fine. And yourself?' Jack didn't normally phone during the day. He usually waited till the weekend when it was cheaper and he knew his mum would be around for a chat.

'Yeah, yeah, fine. I was just – we've got a reading week next week, and I was thinking I might come back and see you.'

'No!' The word came out so quickly it startled them both. 'I mean … aren't you supposed to be studying? Isn't that the point of a reading week?'

His son sounded hurt. 'Well, I'd bring some books back with me. It's fine, my tutor said quite a lot of people go home. And if I need anything else, they'll probably have it at the library in town.'

'Oh, I wouldn't have thought so. I mean, it's specialist books you'll be needing, isn't it? They don't really have … academic stuff.' He was gabbling, searching for excuses.

'Well … I'm sure it'll be fine, anyway.' He sounded doubtful. 'I'd probably just come back for a couple of days. Maybe get the coach down on Tuesday?'

'It's not really convenient, Jack. Your mum'll be working, and you've left it too late for her to arrange any time off. It's their busiest time, the run-up to Christmas. If you'd let us know earlier …' He put a hand over the mouthpiece and held the receiver at arm's length, climbing the first couple of steps to peer round the turn of the stairs at the door to Jack's bedroom. It remained very firmly closed.

'Oh. Well … I guess I won't see you till Christmas, in that case.' His son suddenly sounded like a little boy again, in need of comfort. But in need of protection as well. And that was more important.

'That'll be nice. Yes. It's probably for the best. We don't want you falling behind.' The monstrous noises had started up again, louder than ever. He had to get Jack off the phone before he heard.

'Alright … give my love to Mum, then.'

'Alright. Bye then. Bye.'

As soon as he had got the receiver down the noise reached such a crescendo that he had to sit down at the bottom of the stairs with his eyes shut and his hands clamped tight over his ears to block it out.

Jack didn't phone again until Sunday. Colin was sitting in front of the *Antiques Roadshow* with the sound turned right down when Susan came in from talking to their son, and picked up the remote control and switched it off altogether.

Her eyes looked red and her lips were a thin line. 'You and I are going to have a serious talk,' she said in a voice that was trembling.

Dr Johnson was his favourite out of all the doctors at the unit. She was young, probably only five or six years older than Jack, and she had a way of listening that didn't make you feel like an idiot, no matter what sort of rubbish you came out with. He was glad it was her on duty on his last day there. He wouldn't have liked to leave without saying goodbye.

'So, we've got an appointment set up for you to come back and have a chat to us in the new year, but if you're worried about anything before then, please do give us a call.'

He smiled across the table. 'I will. Don't worry. You've been very helpful.'

'And you're all clear about the medication you're going to be taking?'

He nodded, and she flashed him a lovely reassuring smile. 'As I say, I don't think you'll be needing the Doxepin for more than a few weeks. Once you've got your sleeping patterns back to normal I think you'll start feeling a lot better about things. Try to remember all the stuff we've been through about keeping a bedtime routine, and getting plenty of fresh air and exercise during the day, and everything should be back to normal in no time.' She came round from behind her desk and led him to the door, smiling all the way. Susan was outside in the waiting room – and she had Jack with her, looking rangy and handsome in a blue hooded top and a haircut that could have done with at least a couple of inches off the back. The three of them hugged for a long time, and he had to take a moment and borrow a tissue off Susan before he got himself properly under control and ready to walk out into the bright winter sunshine beyond the clinic doors.

'When did you get back?' he asked his son when they were all in the car and Susan was driving them home.

'Just this morning. Term only finished yesterday. Mum picked me up from the station on the way to meet you.'

'He wanted to be there when you got out,' said Susan as they pulled out onto the ring road. 'I thought we could put the Christmas tree up this afternoon. You and Jack could go to the garden centre and pick us out a nice one.'

'I'd like that,' he said, and swivelled round to smile at his son in the seat behind.

'Run up to the attic and get the decorations down for your dad, would you?' asked Susan while she was tidying away the lunch things. Colin had insisted on going out to have a look under the bonnet of the car, which he reckoned was making a funny noise on the way back from the hospital. 'I've got the ladder in ready: it's leaning against the wall in your room.'

She got distracted while loading the dishwasher, looking through the cupboards and wondering if they had enough food in now that Jack was home for the holiday: she had got used to it being just her over the past fortnight and forgotten how much a nineteen-year-old could put away in a single sitting. Colin came in through the back door while she was counting mince pies. He was rubbing oil off his hands with what looked suspiciously like one of her tea towels. 'I can't see what's wrong with it,' he announced. 'It was due for a service a couple of weeks ago. I don't suppose you remembered, did you?'

'No, I didn't,' she told him. She had had quite enough on her mind.

'Not to worry, I'll give the garage a call. I doubt they'll be able to fit it in before New Year now though.'

There was a cry from upstairs: a sickening yell which echoed all through the house.

'Jack? JACK!' He made it up the stairs in seconds, with Susan not far behind him.

His son's head appeared in the hole that led into the attic, grimacing. 'It's alright, it's just – I think it's a rat. It's OK, it's dead,' he added, seeing his mother's look of horror. 'Been dead for a while, by the look of it. It's gross. Right in the middle of the walkway. I nearly stepped on the bloody thing!'

'Oh, no! How could it have got in?' She turned to her husband, expecting him to share her disgust. But instead he was looking as if he had just got the punch line to a really good joke. 'What are you smiling at?' she asked him.

'Me? Oh, nothing. It's alright, Jack, come down and I'll deal with it. Get me some plastic bags, would you, Sue? And some Flash in a bucket. Look, it's fine. It can't do any harm if it's dead, can it? We'll get Rentokil in in case there are any more. Come on, smile; it's Christmas!'

Whether it was the pills or the counselling she didn't know, but he was on great form for the next few days. He was clearly delighted to have Jack back, and the two of them did everything together, from picking up the tree and the wreath to stringing a new set of outdoor lights in the ornamental cherry on the front lawn. They even stomped across to the Rec when it was already dark one evening to get holly from the big tree beside the cricket pavilion, coming back with great armfuls of the glossy green leaves that they strung up not far off eye level in the hallway, which she thought was taking the carol dangerously literally. But there was no way she was going to complain when they were obviously having such a good time together.

She did complain the following morning when she noticed the set of muddy boot prints that led through the house from the patio door, but the pair of them stood there like naughty schoolboys and swore blind it was nothing to do with them, which was such a blatant cheek that she had to let them off. On Christmas Eve she sent them both round to pick up the turkey while she peeled the sprouts and potatoes in peace with the *Carols from King's*, and the three of them had a drink together before Jack was due to head out and meet his friends in the town. They were going out to the pub, and then on to midnight mass afterwards, which was apparently 'a tradition'. That made her smile. They'd only done it for the first time last year when they were still in sixth form.

It was also, apparently, a tradition to dress up, and Jack came downstairs in a new olive-green shirt she hadn't seen before and one of his dad's ties, looking so handsome that they had to get a photo of him. 'Stand there, in front of the Christmas tree,' she instructed him. 'Left a bit? That's right. Keep still. How does the flash work again? No, it's alright, I've got it.'

She fired off a couple of shots to be sure, the harsh white light bleaching the room and imprinting his silhouette onto her eyelids when she blinked, but she could see that Jack was eager to get away and his increasingly impatient expression was only going to spoil the photos, so she let him go. 'Give us a kiss then,' she told him, and she went to the front door to wave him off and make him repeat his promise that he would look after her car and definitely not have anything more to drink however much his friends tried to persuade him to. 'As if,' he mocked her gently. 'I'm the designated driver: they're all relying on me for lifts home.'

When she got back to the lounge Colin was already settled on the recliner and watching some rubbish on ITV.

'I hope they come out alright,' she said, picking up the camera and making sure she had wound it on properly. 'He looked a bit washed out with the flash. We can finish this film off tomorrow, and then I'll drop it in to Boots when I'm back at work.'

Colin didn't respond. He was half asleep already. They'd been warned the pills could do that.

At least there was one advantage: with him in that state she thought she could risk turning up the thermostat a couple of notches. It had got cold in the house again – she was actually shivering. She wanted to make sure it would be nice and warm for Jack when he got back.

Oh-five-hundred hours, Christmas morning. It is still dark – will be for hours yet, no matter how many excited children are lying awake, willing the sun to rise and reveal the stockings they know have magically appeared at the end of their beds – but the twin beams of the headlights pick out glittering diamonds of hoar frost in the branches of the oak tree that towers over the country lane, and on the leaves of the mistletoe that hunkers in the fork of its branches. In the ditch the reeds are clamped upright, gripped at their base by the glassy sheet that has thawed and refrozen countless times already this winter. Where the bonnet of the car has shattered the ice, a murky brown meniscus has already covered its jagged edges, and the engine has cooled now: the surface of the water will be frozen again by the time the boy is found.

The frost is beginning to reclaim the tyre tracks too: the parallel lines that are etched down the middle of the road, blackening into two smears of cauterised rubber which turn this way, then that, and finally depart from the surface of the road altogether. And already you can barely make out the other marks on the surface of the tarmacadam just ahead of where the car left the road, where a set of army issue boots stood, and scuffed, and stamped, in an attempt to shake out the cramps that are the scourge of any sentry ordered to stand-to in the last black, bleak hours before the dawn.

THE GIFT THAT
KEEPS ON GIVING

DARLING Lucy,
I don't have very long. But I can't go without trying to explain to you. There's so much you still don't know. I can see you rolling your eyes at me when I write that: you think you know everything. You do when you're seventeen. Believe it or not, I remember how it felt. Before life knocked the certainty out of me.

There's one thing I have always been a thousand per cent sure of, though, and that's how I feel about you. From the very first moment I saw your scrunched-up little angry face, bellowing at me as the doctors laid you on my chest, I felt a fierce, fierce love for you. It was so white hot it seemed to burn my insides. And believe me, despite everything that's happened since, I've never stopped feeling it for a single moment. I would do anything for you, my darling. I have done things for you that most mothers would never be able to imagine. And I will again. Because it will keep you safe. And that is the only thing in this world that matters to me.

I know you hate talking about when you were little, but maybe after what has happened tonight – and I am so, so sorry, my darling girl, I wish it could be otherwise – you can understand a little of what it was like. Sitting by the side of your hospital bed, holding on to your tiny hand. Carrying you to the bathroom when you were too weak to make it. You used to protest that you were too big to be carried, and I would pretend to stagger under your weight to make us both laugh, even though you were lighter than a child half your age should have been. Watching how brave and unquestioning you were with the needles and the pills even when I could see how much you had to struggle to swallow them and fight to keep them down, and not being able to promise you that everything was going to be alright because I didn't know whether that was true.

Because by then it had turned out not to be alright so many times. Because you weren't just small for your age. And whatever the chances were, it had turned out not to be nothing. And you weren't bringing up your dinner because of allergies, or gluten, or any of those other things that kids eventually grow out of while their awful, clueless parents loudly talk about 'intolerances' as if they're something to be proud of. And you weren't lucky enough to be one of whatever percentage of kids it is that don't react badly to the chemo, and your hair – your beautiful chestnut hair, with that heartbreaking baby smell I can still summon to my nostrils even now – came out in clumps on the brush that I had to drag over your head as you sat patient and brave on my lap with me trying to avoid your bewildered eyes staring back at me in the mirror. Both of us pretending for each other's sake that this was OK, it was fine, this was just something we were going to get through and come out the other side.

I don't think you've ever known how close you really were to dying. Sure, you used it as a playground boast – 'I nearly died,' I used to hear you saying to your friends after you started hanging out with the sort of kids who think that kind of thing is cool – but it was just words you were using in the way children do, words they've learned the sound of but not the true meaning. That only comes in all its clarity when you're a parent, wide awake in the early hours of the morning and staring sightlessly into the darkness. Or at the emptiness of a long hospital corridor, with its harsh, antiseptic overhead lights melting away all flattery and euphemism to expose the skull beneath the skin.

That was where he found me, all those years ago. I couldn't tell you what day it was, or what time, only that it was an hour when everyone is fast asleep, save for the very best and the very worst in the world.

He looked like just another doctor. He was dressed like a doctor. A surgeon, in fact, though his loose blue scrubs were so spotless and uncreased they made me suddenly aware of my own tired grubbiness and wonder how many days had passed since I had even managed to rub a finger over my teeth or a paper towel beneath my armpits in the Ladies, which was about all I could manage by way of hygiene at that point. But he was a lot younger than Dr Woodville, the surgeon who did your first operation, and who had assured me that they had almost certainly succeeded in locating all of the tumours and there was a very good chance little Lucy would be up and about in no time, something else that turned out to be more empty words. And he didn't look much like the junior doctors I'd seen dragging themselves from ward to ward in the early hours either. His face was as fresh and unlined as an airbrushed model in a magazine, not a strand of his slick black hair was out of place, and he had the most incredible green eyes that seemed to look right into me as he sat down opposite and asked the only question that mattered.

'How is she tonight?'

It took me by surprise. You'd be amazed how many people in those weeks had come up to me to ask me, 'Are you alright?' even though most of them had more than

enough medical qualifications to know there was no possible way I could be. I gave him as much of an answer as
I could fit into words: that you were sleeping. Pure exhaus-
tion was doing at last what the drugs no longer seemed
able to. And I was trying to make myself comfortable –
no, that's another empty phrase, I was slumped on a hard
plastic chair trying to relish how uncomfortable I was,
because that way I could kid myself I was somehow taking
some of your suffering for myself, even though I knew the
world doesn't work like that, however much it ought to.

Except that night it turned out maybe it can.

'Dr Ramakrishnan is a very good doctor,' he told me.
That was the paediatric oncologist in charge of your treatment. 'I'm sure she's doing all that she can for Lucy.'

I could barely hear my own voice as I trotted out another
of my practised phrases. 'Everyone's been wonderful.'

He nodded, and he seemed to know that I couldn't
manage a conversation, so we just sat together for a while.
I suppose, looking back, that was another thing that should
have given me a clue he wasn't a junior doctor, because
when do they have the time to just sit around? But right
then what I needed most was the company of someone
who seemed to understand, and I was long past asking
questions. After a bit I realised I was crying, and he took
out a handkerchief – a proper, white cotton handkerchief,
folded neatly into quarters, then diagonally again to fit in

his breast pocket – and passed it over to me as I nodded my thanks, and we sat there in the corridor opposite each other, the only sounds my sniffling and the quiet hum through the door of the machines that were keeping you alive.

After some time had passed he leaned forward, steepling his fingers – he had long fingers, I remember, with perfectly manicured nails – and looked at me like he had come to a decision.

'There is … one thing we haven't tried yet for Lucy.'

It was as if a little jarring jolt of hope had gone off somewhere deep inside me, where I thought nothing was left but emptiness. I suddenly felt more awake than I think I have ever been. 'What? What is it?'

He explained that it was an experimental treatment. Not one that was on offer to everyone. And that there was a risk involved. But I wasn't interested in any of that. If it gave you a chance, I would take any risk there was.

He asked me if anyone had talked to me about donors. Of course they had. Even back then you could barely get out of a GP surgery without them trying to push one of the little red and blue cards on you. But they had also told me it would be no use in your case, even though I had said again and again how happy I would be to give up any or all of my own organs in place of your tiny ones as the tumours worked their way through each of them in turn. And I told him as much, again.

He gave me an apologetic smile. 'I'm afraid that wouldn't be suitable in this case. The process does not leave the donor in a … functioning state. And Lucy would need you after the treatment to look after her and nurse her back to health. Unless … there's anyone else?'

The tears were coming back again. His handkerchief was soaked through. 'I'm on my own.'

'Ah. Lucy's father isn't …?'

I shook my head. He nodded sympathetically. 'Naturally it's every parent's first instinct to do anything for their child. To be prepared to give up everything for them. At least, that's how it should be.'

It felt like I was being given hope, only to have it snatched away from me. Although at least now I had someone to blame for it.

I told him all about your dad. How we hadn't had any contact with him in years. How you didn't even remember him. I told him things I've never told you, my love, although I think you always understood more than you let on. I always wanted to protect you from the details. But you need to know them now. To understand.

Your dad and I met too young. And although I've never regretted it for a second, we definitely had you too young. When you're only a teenager you've barely got enough love for yourself, let alone anyone else, and your dad had a big problem even liking himself. I don't even know what he thought he felt for me. And then you arrived, and there was never any question where all the love I had to share was going. Which I suppose, looking back, left him feeling even more on the outside, just like he was always saying he did. But that's not to make any excuses for him. He made more than enough of those for himself.

I should have spotted the signs so much earlier than I did. On our second or third date he tried to batter some lads from the college rugby team who were making laddish remarks at me in the bar, but somehow at the time I made myself think it was romantic – my own knight in armour, defending my honour. Except that after he came off the worse in the encounter, and I was left doing DIY first aid in my bedroom because he flatly refused to go to A&E, he somehow managed to turn it back on me and tell me that he wouldn't have had to risk a kicking on my behalf if it wasn't for the way I dressed and acted. And after it happened a few more times I started to believe him, which is why I started wearing all those drab jeans and baggy T-shirts you used to laugh at in my old photos. But I never minded you laughing: you were right, they were terrible, and old-fashioned even then, and secretly I love the fact that you were once interested enough to want to look at them.

But gradually I realised that I was growing apart from my friends, and stopping doing the things I used to love to do – do you remember years ago how amazed you were when I told you I used to act in the drama society at college, and you said, You? No way! I kept telling myself that it was just part of growing up and discovering who I really was, when actually I was being turned into the person he wanted me to be. Only it turned out he didn't like her much, either.

And then I got pregnant. You don't want or need to know the details, but it's the reason I've tried damn hard all your life to make sure you're not the sort of girl who'd let something like that happen to her. And he insisted he had to drop out of college and get a job to support me while I carried on studying, and then devoted himself full-time to resenting me for both those things.

You know he used to hit me, because I've been honest about that ever since you first traced the scar on my fore-head with a tiny finger and asked me in a solemn voice how it got there. But the bit I couldn't explain to you, because as a child you wouldn't understand, was that it wasn't the violence that hurt the most. It was the way he always looked at me and talked to me. Like I was some kind of vermin that had somehow got into his house and was fouling the place up. Something like a slug that however successfully it manages to stay hidden and out of your way can't help but leave a disgusting trail behind so you know it's been there. The slaps and pushes and dragging grips on the arm only happened when he had been drinking, and I got to be an expert at spotting the signs and finding excuses for getting you out of the flat then, whatever time of the day or night it might be. But that look – that contempt – that was there was there all the time. And I lived with it right up until one day when I came into the front room when you were playing happily in your playpen, gurgling away without a care in the world, and I saw him looking at you with exactly the same expression. He didn't do anything else, just sat there looking down at you in utter disgust and resentment, but the very next morning, as soon as he left for work, I packed a bag for you and one for me and walked out of that grotty little flat and never once looked back.

I told the stranger this, and much, much more, right there in the hospital corridor. The words just came tumbling out of me, maybe because I'd been keeping them pent up inside for so long. And by the time I'd finished he couldn't have been in any doubt about exactly how I felt about your – no, he doesn't deserve to be called your dad, he never did anything to earn that title.

At least, he never did until that night.

I said I didn't even know where he was these days. It had been years since I'd heard anything about him. His mother knew better than to include any mention of him in the Christmas cards she sent each year if she wanted there to be a chance of you getting to read them.

He reassured me that wasn't a problem. 'We never have a problem finding donors. Our register is very comprehensive. All we need is your consent to proceed.'

I could kid myself that I didn't know what I was signing up for, that he somehow tricked me into it, took advantage of my vulnerable state. But we talked for a long time that night. And I understood completely.

He held out his hand, and I passed him the wringing-wet handkerchief. He took it, and he folded it up neatly like before, but before he tucked it back into his pocket he pressed it hard to his lips, and those green eyes were looking right into mine the whole time.

'Go in and see your daughter,' he told me, and I nodded dumbly. My legs had stiffened beneath me and it took me a moment to find my balance and cross to the door of the room where you were still sleeping soundly, the machines beeping and whirring around you. And when I turned to look back, the long hospital corridor stretched away empty in both directions.

You stayed asleep for a long time that night, and well into the next morning, and when you woke up you looked more refreshed than you had in weeks, with a little colour creeping back into your cheeks. Your test results still weren't good, but by the next day they had crept up, and they carried on rising all that week until Dr Ramakrishnan gave the first genuine smile I think I'd ever seen her give and told me you really did seem to be making progress. By then you had managed to sit up and eat a whole meal – chicken pie and vegetables, I'll always remember – and most of your jelly for afters, and the nurses were so pleased with you that they even managed to persuade me to go home and sleep in my own bed for a night, and when I got back not long after seven the next morning they were laughing and telling me I wasn't going to believe it, but you'd already had your breakfast as well.

From then on there was no stopping you. You were scooting around the place on a walking frame before we knew it, making friends with the kids on the other wards, and getting cross with me if I tried to go into the bathroom with you because you said you didn't need me any more. After a few weeks I was taking you off the ward every afternoon for walks in the park, or out for pizzas, or trips to the cinema, whatever you demanded. The mornings were taken up with talking to doctors and social workers about the care and support package we would need in order to have you home for Christmas. We managed it, too. And after that, except for regular outpatient check-ups that became less and less frequent as the years went by, you never went back.

In the midst of it all I was too busy to notice we didn't get a card from Nana Barnes that year. She wrote me a letter towards the end of January, to say sorry but she had some bad news: her son had passed away. He had been found with knife wounds in an alley behind a pub in Portsmouth, where he'd apparently been living. The police thought he must have got into a fight with someone – he'd been barred from the place earlier in the evening, which sounded like him – but they didn't have any suspects, and they thought in the end it wasn't the stabbing that killed him: he froze to death out there by the bins. She said that although she understood how things were, she thought I would want to be told.

She was wrong. I didn't want to know at all.

I put the letter away. I wasn't such an irresponsible mother that I wasn't going to tell you, but with everything else that was going on you didn't need to know right then. And somehow, like a lot of other things, I never did get round to telling you. So that's what this letter is for now. To make sure you have the full picture. You might have stopped listening a long time ago to anything I say, but you at least deserve to have my side of the story.

When people ask me how the teenage years are going, I tend to say things like 'Ooh, we have our ups and downs.' But we can't kid ourselves, can we, Lucy? There have been a lot more downs than ups, especially lately. At first I was so relieved and happy just to have you home and well again that I didn't see it, or I told myself you were catching up on all the things you'd missed out on because of your illness, and everything would settle down. And of course, I blamed myself, for all the usual reasons single mums do, convincing myself there was something missing in your upbringing that should have been there. But that wasn't true. It was actually the opposite, wasn't it?

'She's got the devil in her, that one,' my mum once said in exasperation after you'd pushed her right to her limit. It was after that awful incident with the kitten that you insisted till you were blue in the face was an accident, and we said we believed you because we wanted to so much. But it wasn't the devil. And I know, because, god forgive me, it was me that put it there.

I wasn't sure at first. Not for a long time. I made excuses for your behaviour, apologising endlessly to the parents of other kids at your school, begging your teachers for extra chances and pleading special circumstances right up until you got yourself permanently excluded. And I made excuses for the bruises too, hardly believing the same words could be coming out of my mouth again. You were so little when it started. I told myself you were just lashing out, that you didn't know your own strength.

Maybe you didn't. Is that how it works, Lucy? Is there still a frightened little girl somewhere in there, terrified of the brute she's forced to share a body with and unable to control him? Is that maybe the reason for the boozing, and now the drugs? Are you trying to blot him out, escape from him?

If that is the case, I can't blame you. I don't resent the money you've stolen from me over the years to pay for it all. I'd gladly hand it over, and more. Because the alternative is even more awful. If that's just you, telling the truth, that means you really do hate me. That I'm worthless, the worst mother in the world. And I know that's not right.

And so will you, now. I'm proving it to you.

This shows you how much I've been clutching at straws lately, but I even thought Charlie might be the one to save you. Because I could see how much you cared about him. Alright, I don't think much of him – you could do a lot better than a drug dealer, and I know that's what he is, Lucy, I'm not stupid, however often you tell me I am. And I hate the way he's treated our home like a dosshouse from the very first time you brought him back, and me like the hired skivvy, but I suppose he was only picking that up from you. And I wouldn't trust him not to hurt you, or cheat on you, or break your heart sooner or later. But there was one time, when I got back from a late shift and found the pair of you passed out on the sofa in the front room in a stinking haze of weed, and the look you had on your face while you were cradled in his arms was one I thought I'd never see again. You looked happy. Content. So full of trust. I'd forgotten you could even look that way.

It was the same expression you used to have when I was carrying you in the hospital all those years ago. And for once it made me not mind that you'd used up all the food I'd got in for my dinner and most of it was crusted onto the pans and the plates with half-crushed spliff ends in them that were left scattered all over the kitchen for me to clear up as usual.

So you were so wrong when you screamed at me after the accident that you hoped I was happy now. Yes, I was always going on about his motorbike and how dangerous it was, especially when he was stoned, but surely you can see that was because I knew something like this might happen? And when I said thank god you weren't on the bike too, that was pure relief speaking. And when you yelled at me that you wished you had been, that if he died you would rather be dead too, it was like a knife going into me. Because I could tell that you actually meant it.

So what I'm telling you, Lucy, is I get it. I understand. And you have my blessing. Because you see I came back after the nurses told me it would be best for me to leave. I waited outside the Casualty department at the edge of the car park, watching the ambulances come and go, until I thought you'd have had enough time to calm down. Until after the last of the drunks had been bandaged up and sent home, and the waiting room had emptied, and the nurses had gone off their night shift and the cleaners arrived, though the sky was still black as could be. And then I crept back. I got as far as the doors, stopping just outside the circle of light that spilled out of them, not close enough to trigger the sensor that sets them sliding open. I looked in through the glass, and I saw you sitting there with your back to me, looking so vulnerable, and so young, and so broken. And I saw who was sitting there opposite you. He was dressed just the same as before. And when he spotted me, his green eyes locking on mine over your shoulder as you sobbed into that neatly folded handkerchief, I realised something else. He hadn't aged by a single day.

I know how it works, Lucy. It has to be someone you've loved. He explained that to me too. Otherwise everyone would be doing it, wouldn't they? If you could just pick some awful criminal, or a politician, and wipe them out just like that to save someone who mattered, think how much better the world could be. But that would be too easy. No, it has to be someone who cared for you, who did their best to love you in their own way, even if they didn't always get it right. And it also has to be someone who you're now prepared to sacrifice without a second thought.

And I accept it. I'll go happily. Because I know I can make you safe, my darling girl. Charlie may not be all you need him to be, or love you as much as you need him to, but I can. I can straighten him out, make him behave like he ought to. With me pushing him, he can become the man that's good enough for you. Who can save you from yourself.

And I won't ever have to let you go.

That was a knock. It's him, or maybe his people. I must go and open the door to them.

I don't know how it will happen. I think we will go for a walk together, somewhere far away from the house. It's a cold night again, but I won't bother with a coat. I will leave this letter here on the kitchen table for you. You sit tight at the hospital and wait for news of Charlie. It shouldn't be too long now.

I will see you very soon, my darling girl.

AFTERLIFE

I started writing these ghost stories to send to friends and family in place of Christmas cards in 2005 and have kept up the tradition (almost) every winter solstice since. So I owe an enormous and obvious debt to the don of the genre, M.R. James, who delivered his ghost stories to his selected favourites in his rooms at Cambridge each Christmas Eve.

But to amuse myself (and hopefully some of the recipients who actually bothered to open the email attachments over the years), I included deliberate little homages to other writers along the way – seasonably inappropriate Easter eggs, you might call them – as well as wearing my influences on my sleeve as boldly as the reindeer on a Christmas jumper. You may have spotted one or two of them along the way.

Don't worry, they're not like Pokémon: you don't have to catch them all. But this collection would not and could not exist were it not for:

Robert Aickman, Joan Aiken, Clive Barker, Julia Bell, Emily Brontë, Angela Carter, Aidan Chambers, Mark Z. Danielewski, Drew and John Erick Dowdle, Peter Firmin, Neil Gaiman, Alan Garner, Edward Gorey, Edward Grey, the Brothers Grimm, Peter Haining, Robin Hardy, Robert A. Heinlein, W.W. Jacobs, Tina Jackson, Tove Jansson, James Joyce, Stephen King, Nigel Kneale, Andrew Lang, C.S. Lewis, Ian Livingstone, H.P. Lovecraft, Robert Lumley, Will Maclean, Ruth Manning-Sanders, Daphne du Maurier, Carey Miller, Alan Moore, Ursula Moray Williams, Wilfred Owen, E. Nesbit, Charles Perrault, Oliver Postgate, Anthony Read, Talbot Rothwell, Dan Rhodes, Anthony Shaffer, Julian Simpson, Andrew Smith, Christopher Smith, Catherine Storr, Vera Southgate, Milton Subotsky, Alan Temperley, Elizabeth Warren, Joss Whedon, John Wyndham.

Seek out their work. Devour it. Let them live on …